Waiting for Eternity

ALYSON ROOT

J&M Books

For permission requests, write to a.rootauthor@alysonroot.com

Published by J&M Books

Lytchett House, 13 Freeland Park, Wareham Road, Poole, Dorset, BH16 6FA

Print ISBN: 978-1-917785-08-2

Ebook ISBN: 978-1-917785-26-6

Developmental Edit & Cover design by:

Tara Sullivan, The Write Gal Co.

www.thewritegal.com

Proofread By:

Crystal Lee Wren, COLProof

"If I had to choose between breathing or loving you, I would say 'I love you' with my last breath."
—Shannon Dermott

One

Amelia once told me that she felt a weight settle on her the day she turned twenty-nine. It was the day she heard the metaphorical clock of her existence start to tick down. Until today, I never fully understood what she meant.

And yet, here I am on my twenty-ninth birthday feeling the same weight, hearing the same ticking. Although, there is one difference. Amelia was waiting to fall into madness. Convinced she would never find her mate. I'm waiting and praying that my body will accept the changes necessary to be one with Amelia for all eternity. There are still three hundred and sixty-five days to go until we have an answer. What's one more year when we have already endured two together? Blissfully happy, yet all the while, an undercurrent of anxiety is in constant motion between us.

If the change doesn't happen or my body can't handle it, Amelia will be alone for the rest of her existence. My soul cries out in agony at the mere thought of it.

I was taken by Amelia from the first second I saw her. Even though she pissed me the hell off by stepping behind my bar. Of course, I had no idea who she was at the time. Imagine my surprise when I learned she was the owner of the club I was working at.

Also, imagine my surprise at how enamored I was, even though I was dating someone else. I couldn't help it, though. Amelia Loch snagged me in seconds. I suppose the shock of finding out Amelia's true nature should have changed everything. I think it would have for most people, but for me it made no difference in how I felt about her.

The time we spent getting acquainted was all I needed to know my heart belonged to her. The fact she drinks blood is neither here nor there for me—a fact which surprised Amelia. She'd expected me to run for the hills screaming, but there was no way. If anything, I loved her more. Her beauty is ethereal. She's smart and hardworking. The fact she can pick me up like I'm a rag doll only adds to the ecstasy I feel around her. I've never once felt scared of her or any of her family, who have welcomed me with open arms.

Our mating was hard and emotional. It broke me to know she'd suffered such terrible side effects because of her feelings for me, but I understood why she kept it a secret. Our bond had to happen organically. Amelia understood that I couldn't force myself to fall in love with her. Lucky for us both, I fell in love with her easily.

I still get chills when I recall our mating. The sheer elation I felt as my soul reached out and entwined with hers. Nothing in this world could ever compare to that.

The night of Amelia's thirtieth birthday is at the forefront of my mind as I sit here celebrating with my loved ones. We held our breath at the stroke of midnight for her. Although we bonded, there was always a sliver of worry that Amelia may fall into madness as her cells changed.

The event passed with little fanfare. Amelia didn't want a fuss. Well, when I say there was little fanfare, that's not entirely true. Amelia asked me to be her wife, and of course I said yes. We agreed that the wedding should wait until I turned thirty. One year. And then I can marry my mate. Or I die. Or nothing happens and I remain human. I'm not sure which would be worse.

"Are you enjoying yourself, my love?" Amelia's velvet voice caresses me and I shiver.

Two years have passed, but the effect she has on me has only intensified. I look at her, my eyes gliding over her lithe body. Amelia Loch is a goddess. Her body elicits such want, I struggle to keep myself under control. Her hair is as black as a moonless night, and naturally pin straight. She styles it into perfect waves when she wants to impress—not that it would take much for her to make an impression on anyone. I love it when she leaves it down, as she has this evening. Her dress is a midnight blue with a slit up both thighs. She is delectable, and she is mine. I see the wanting looks cast her way every time we enter a room, but Amelia's attention never wavers.

People can surround us, and yet I know her gaze is always on me. I feel her presence wherever I am. That is part of our bond, our everlasting connection.

Turning toward her in my seat, I stroke her cheek. "I'm having a wonderful night. Thank you for this."

We are floating a few miles off the coast of LA on the Loch family yacht—a luxurious behemoth befitting the Loch's sizable wealth with dozens of cabins to house our guests and a private chef catering our every whim. It still takes me aback every time I step on board. All my friends and family are celebrating my birthday. Humans and vampires alike. My parents and friends have no idea the Lochs are non-human. I've discussed how to handle it with Amelia several times.

Once I change, I will stop aging, just like Amelia. My parents aren't stupid. They will question things as they grow old and I remain a fresh-faced thirty-year-old. Even though we've had the discussion, we haven't come up with a suitable way to tell them. I can't be certain they won't freak out.

Considering all that, it's possible I won't see them as often in the future. The Loch family has been in LA for nearly forty years. We will probably have to move away, so as not to cause any unwanted attention to the fact none of the Lochs look over fifty. Fun fact, Harlan and Victoria are over two hundred years old. Of all the things I came to learn the day Amelia outed herself to me, that was what surprised me the most. I don't know why.

"Are you sure? You look lost in thought."

"Honestly, honey, I'm good. Just taking a breath. My family is a lot." I laugh before placing a tender kiss on Amelia's lips.

"Erin, Lord above, I've been looking for you. Your cousin, Parker? I think that's her name, won't leave me alone." Dana Brooks stands in front of me, just as beautiful as always. Dana is Amelia's friend and former lover.

"It's your own fault," I joke. "You turned on the charm and now you have to deal with the consequences."

Dana is polyamorous. She's married, but I don't believe I have ever seen her without a lover or two on the side.

"I can't help that I'm irresistible." Her signature smirk makes me laugh.

"Just tell her you're married. Where is David, anyway?"

"Working, darling, as usual."

"And little Aurora?"

Dana's daughter has just turned one. She is angelic and stirs up mushy feelings inside me. I want children, as does Amelia, but once again, we must wait until I change.

"With Giselle. She's finally getting into a sleeping pattern, and I didn't want to disturb it."

Giselle is Dana's au pair. Very striking and a little terrifying, if I'm honest. Actually, I think even Dana is scared of her. She hasn't tried to bed her at all.

"I'll talk to Parker," I say. "Maybe go hide for a few minutes."

Rolling her eyes, Dana stalks off.

"Excuse me, honey, I'll be back soon." Standing, I go to leave, but Amelia pulls me toward her. The kiss she settles on my lips, steals my breath.

"Damn," I exhale when she lets me go. Walking off on unsure legs, I spot my cousin immediately and I can tell she's searching for Dana.

"Erin, have you seen that rather delicious cop?"

Dana planned to change careers a few years ago, but she couldn't bring herself to leave the force. All she needed was a long vacation before she was back to harassing Amelia on her Ducati with lights and sirens. I can't say I mind. Amelia is a speed demon and needs reigning in once in a while.

"Yes, I have, and she's in hiding." I laugh because the whole thing is amusing. Dana thought she could charm Parker's pants off, like she has so many others. What she didn't realize was that Parker is just as much a womanizer as she is. Parker loves a challenge and Dana skulking off has lit a fire under her ass.

"She's hiding. Oh, how lovely!" The gleam in Parker's eyes makes me laugh harder.

"You know what...have at it. She went into the galley."

Parker throws me a wink and strides off.

"You're going to hell for that." Amelia chuckles in my ear. Her strong arms wrap around my waist.

"Dana loves it." I quip.

"And I love you."

I turn in her arms, encircling her neck. We sway to the music, even though the dance floor is clear across the room. When we're together, nothing else exists. I'm sure many would find that unhealthy, but they haven't given their soul to another. They could never understand.

"What time can we skip out of here?" I whisper in her ear because I know it drives her nuts.

"I thought you were enjoying yourself."

"Oh, I am. I'm just ready to unwrap my birthday present," I mumble against her lips.

"Mmm, I like that idea." She pulls me closer. "We'll give it another twenty minutes and take our leave."

We are going to devour each other.

Stepping out of Amelia's embrace, I put a few feet of space between us.

"I'm going to speak to my parents." My voice is breathy because my body is still responding to her. I want to rip her out of that dress and bury my head between her legs. Amelia's eyes sparkle as she gleams my thoughts. It's a new ability we've developed.

8

When we first bonded, even unofficially, we felt each other's presence. Ever since Amelia became immortal, we can hear snippets of one another's thoughts. Usually, when emotions are strong.

Right now, my emotions are pulsing with desire, and Amelia knows it.

"Go, speak with your family. I'm not going anywhere."

A frisson of love courses through my chest. I'm not sure I can wait another twenty minutes.

My parents are laughing as I approach. They have become extremely friendly with Amelia's parents, who are the epitome of smooth and charming.

"Mom, are you having fun?"

"Erin love, there you are. Victoria and I were just talking about how we should start planning your wedding."

"I told you we're waiting a little while."

"Yes, I know, I know. But you're my baby and I'm excited."

Pulling her in, I squeeze hard. God, what do I do if they can't accept Amelia, her family, and, by extension, me? I've always been close to my parents. For the most part, they let me live my life. I was free to make decisions, even bad ones. They wanted me to learn and grow into a strong and independent woman. They weren't quite so liberal-thinking when I quit college to tend bar, but the years have softened their views. If I'm happy, they're happy. I just hope that still applies after they know the truth.

"I'm excited too, Mom. As is Victoria. And yes, you're right, we should start planning."

I see the quick side glance from Victoria, but I ignore it. Even if things don't go to plan on my thirtieth birthday, I still intend to marry Amelia. I will be with her for as long as I can, even though it will cause us both significant pain in the end.

Having my future rest solely on the stories of old causes me anxiety. Barty and Anya are the only successful pair we know of, but that doesn't mean there weren't more attempts. What if history is littered with the bodies of unsuccessfully mated vampire and human couples, all of who tasted each other's blood?

There is no guarantee, even if Dr. Mendhi claims, my blood is already affected. And what if I do change? Can my body handle such a radical shift? For the last two years, I've suffered repeated nightmares of my bones cracking under the strain of cellular changes.

I can't help but worry about our bond, too. Will it survive as-is? Or is there a chance *I* could fall into madness?

Too many questions and too little time to figure out the answers.

"Now, I hope you don't mind, but I'm getting a little tired. I think I'll retire. I'm getting old, ya know."

The group laughs, and none of them buys my excuse for one second. Especially when Amelia scoops me into her arms and marches out with me. I can't help but giggle at the wolf whistles and chants that follow us out the door. Burying my head in Amelia's soft neck, I inhale her scent. My body is already trembling in anticipation.

Amelia pushes open our bedroom door and flings me to the bed. My panties are soaked with need. Closing the door with her foot, Amelia stalks toward me in that dress. My mouth salivates.

Two

Amelia runs her hands slowly up my legs, starting from my ankles. Her gaze is locked on me as her hands snake closer to where I want them. My eyelids draw closed under the weight of lust.

Reaching out, I try to grab her. I want to feel her powerful body on mine, but Amelia resists.

"Not yet, my love. Just relax and enjoy feeling me touch you."

Something inside me stirs. A dislike of being denied what is rightfully mine.

"I want to touch you, too. I want to rip that dress off. But you can keep the heels on."

I'm not sure where this need to take charge of our lovemaking is coming from. But there is almost a burning desire to claim my position.

Amelia lets out a low, sultry chuckle. "My, my, aren't you feisty this evening, my queen."

"Amelia," I warn. Calling me her queen ignites my body with a fierce heat.

"Erin," she replies playfully. "I have plans for you. Will you let me carry on, or would you prefer to keep chatting?" She lifts one of her raven eyebrows. Her dark eyes bore into mine and I'm ready to do whatever the hell she wants.

"I'm yours."

In every way possible.

"Good, now stay still. I want to feast on you with my eyes before I fuck you into next week."

Amelia's eyes take in every inch of me. Slowly, she lifts my hips, sliding my dress up. I arch my back, allowing her to take the dress up further. I hear her exhale in appreciation of my body. I shiver, knowing what's to come.

In a second, my dress is thrown to the floor.

"Oh, I like this." Amelia traces my body with an index finger. She lingers over my breasts. I chose a forest green set, knowing she likes me in that color. "Bra stays on."

The feel of air hitting my pussy tells me my panties are probably on the floor with my dress.

"Now, watch." She commands.

My eyes never leave Amelia, who stands, unzips her dress and lets it fall to the floor. My gaze travels from her eyes to her perfect breasts, down to her perfect sex. She's been commando all evening. My legs spread automatically, making her smile.

I watch her walk away to our luggage. Biting my lip, I try to suppress an excited squeal. Oh Christ, I know what she's brought with her and I can't wait. After a few seconds of rustling, Amelia turns to face me. Hanging between her legs is the custom-made vibrating dildo she commissioned for us. It's gold and blue, the same colors we both saw the night we mated.

Walking back to me in her heels, the toy swinging slightly, I have to clench my thighs back together to stop myself from getting too excited. Amelia has brought me to orgasm before without even touching me.

Her palms slide over my thighs, all the way to my hips. Suddenly, Amelia pulls me until my legs dangle over the edge of the bed. Once again, her hands are on my legs. This time traveling down to my ankles. Hoisting both my legs into the air and over her shoulders. Thank god I'm flexible.

She's looking down at me with hunger in her eyes. With her hands still on my ankles, she spreads me wide. I am completely open to her. Finally, her gaze shifts from my face to my soaked folds. I am so ready.

Using my abs, I lift my upper body slightly so I can reach the toy. Guiding the head to my entrance, I plead with her silently to fuck me. The moment my back hits the mattress again, she plunges into me, gripping my ankles tighter.

Yes, worship me!

I raise my hands to the headboard and hold on. My body sways with every thrust, my breasts moving to the rhythm. Amelia fixes her eyes on them, holding her bottom lip between her teeth.

Our breathing becomes labored as we glide toward climax. Suddenly, the dildo vibrates. God love Amelia for adding a pressure timer. As far as I know, this is a one-off design. We should tell people how fucking fantastic it is.

When Amelia first told me about the add-on, I was nonplussed. We've got a trunk full of toys that vibrate. What was another one? But then she explained the moment she enters me; the toy registers the external pressure. The timer is set to two minutes, giving us time to get into a rhythm. Then it vibrates until pulled out. I'm not nonplussed anymore. It's the best toy we have ever used.

Amelia's thrusts grow urgent. Her eyes are still on my breasts. Mine are on the toy sliding in and out of me. I see how stretched I am, and it adds to my excitement. The first tendrils of an orgasm wind from my core. I feel myself clench around the dildo as I succumb to its will. I can't hold on any longer. My voice echoes around our cabin. I hear myself scream Amelia's name. Blue and gold lights dance around us as our climaxes crash through us both. Amelia's whole body is shaking, and an almost pained moan filters through the noise of my own.

We are sweating and sated. The toy stops vibrating the moment it leaves me. I hear it clunk to the floor and then feel Amelia's body lazily drape over me. My arms pull her closer, my face buried in her neck once more.

"Happy birthday, my love," she pants.

A giggle escapes me in a stuttered release. "Best. Birthday. Ever."

I'm sure the entire boat heard us, but I'm unfazed. I could never be embarrassed about making love with Amelia. We lay silent for several minutes, catching our breaths.

"Have you noticed the lights are brighter?" I'm referring to the blue and gold lights we see as we orgasm.

"Yes. I wondered if you'd noticed."

"I wonder why?"

"Maybe because we're getting closer to your thirtieth?" Amelia's voice is soft and sleepy.

"Mmm." I feel myself drift off. It's one more thing we need to talk about.

The bed is empty when I wake, per usual. Amelia has always been an early riser. I'm sure to find her at the table with the rest of her family. They are the definition of early birds, a nest of Larks rising at dawn like clockwork. I'm an owl, through and through.

I stretch my body, feeling every muscle. My calves hurt from being straightened for so long. I'm flexible, but not the day after it would seem. An invigorating shower wakes me up enough to dress and head to the family table. As suspected, I find the Loch family already there, flasks of Red in front of each of them. The seat next to Amelia is for me. I greet everyone and tuck in. I'm starving. I notice the sly smiles and winks from Amelia's siblings. I'm surprised Lucille hasn't sai—

"You know, you should gift us all ear plugs. I'm tired of having to stuff mine with tissue every time you go at it." Lucille is feeling pleased with herself. Amelia rolls her eyes. She is much better at letting Lucille's gibes roll off her back now. They fought like cats and dogs when we first met.

"Don't cover your ears, dear sister. You might learn something." Amelia takes a dainty sip of Red as she speaks. Lucas, the youngest, almost spits his drink across the table.

"Burn." He laughs. I roll my lips, trying not to laugh.

"Children." Victoria sighs, but her eyes crinkle in amusement.

"She started it," Amelia shoots. Okay, so she still lets Lucille get to her. I lay my hand on her thigh and she immediately relaxes.

"Erin, dear, were you serious about organizing the wedding?" Victoria is ignoring Amelia and Lucille, who are shooting daggers at each other.

"Yes, I think it's time."

"I thought you wanted to wait until..." Victoria gestures with her hands instead of saying the words.

"I don't see the point. Whatever happens next year, I want to be married to Amelia."

The table grows quiet.

"You want to marry before your birthday?" Amelia is looking at me with pinched eyebrows. I'd hoped we would have this discussion in private, but what the hell.

"Yes, honey, I do."

"But—"

"But what? We are mated. I'm yours and you're mine. No matter what happens, whether I change or..."

Amelia swallows thickly, hating it when I talk about the possibility of dying. I understand, but we can't run away from it. All indications point to me successfully becoming a vampire, but I will only be the second human in history to do so. It's not a guarantee.

I forge on. "Whatever. I want to be married to you."

"I agree," Harlan pipes up. He's a man of few words but always speaks up when something is important. "No matter what the future holds, you should celebrate your love. A wedding is just what you need."

"Amelia?" She is quiet. I know she needs a few minutes to process.

"I'd marry you right here, right now, Erin Hanson." She leans in and kisses me thoroughly.

"Well, that settles it," Laurence, the eldest sibling, announces. "We have a wedding to plan!"

"We?" Amelia asks, amused.

"Yes, we. It's a family affair."

I love how indignant he sounds, as if the very idea of the family not being involved in the planning is utterly ridiculous. Laurence has always played a father figure with Amelia, even if unwarranted.

"Fine, I suppose we'll let you chip in, now and then."

Shaking my head and grinning, I get back to my food, leaving the Loch siblings to squabble amongst themselves.

"Any thoughts on the location?" Aliah asks.

Honestly, I wouldn't mind a simple ceremony with just close friends and family, but I know how long Amelia's family has waited for this day. A day they never thought they would get to celebrate.

"We'd like something small and intimate." Amelia looks at me and I know she's just heard my thoughts. "Just friends and family."

"Well, that won't—" Victoria begins, but Harlan cuts her off.

"This isn't our day, Victoria. If they want it small, they can have it small."

I smile at him appreciatively.

"I'd like to have a beach wedding." Preferably one in Hawaii.

"I'll see if the resort is available." Amelia kisses me on the cheek before taking out her phone.

"What resort?" Lucille is easily irritated when she feels left out of the loop.

"The one in Hawaii," I answer, as Amelia steps away to make the call.

"Oh fuck, you can do that mind-reading thing, can't you?" Lucille groans.

I look at her, perplexed. Is it not normal for every mated pair to read each other's moods and thoughts?

"I'm guessing by the look on your face that you thought it was a common thing," Victoria says. I nod. "It's not. Harlan and I are able to communicate silently, but as far as I know, none of our other children and their mates can." She casts a glance around the table, looking for confirmation. Several heads shake. "No, so it seems you and Amelia are the only ones."

"Wow, okay." I'm not really sure what to say to that. Does that mean something?

"Can you have full conversations?" Marcus asks. Marcus and Amelia are close. They share the same outlook on many things.

"Mostly just snippets of thoughts. More so when we feel powerful emotions."

"You'll find it will develop over time. Harlan and I can converse quite easily."

"We know." Amelia sits back at the table, placing her phone in her pocket. "It was extremely annoying growing up. You'd both just sit there silently and leave us guessing."

Harlan bellows out a deep laugh. "We sometimes did it just for kicks."

"It has a downside too, though." Victoria arches an eyebrow at her husband. "There are some things you just don't want to know. Things that should remain private."

"I don't think I want to know what she means by that," Amelia mumbles in my ear, causing me to chuckle softly.

"Arguments are also a time when hearing your partner's thoughts can be troublesome." Victoria and Harlan look lovingly at each other. I wonder how many times they've had to resolve a fight that spiraled out of control because they could read each other's minds.

"My advice," Harlan says, turning to us. "Never go to bed angry. Even if one of you hears something you don't like, talk it out. No matter what was said or thought. You are soulmates until the end."

Three

Insomnia is crazy tonight. I'm on my third shift of the week. Amelia grumbles now and then that I work too much. It's laughable, really, she's as bad as me. We both love the club business. I was over the moon when she opened a sister club in New York. I was positively bowled over when she revealed the name. Eriu: it's the oldest word for Erin in Latin, which means Ireland. Fitting, really.

I was even more surprised to find out Amelia had gifted me part of the business. Both Insomnia and Eriu. Claire, the club's manager, was made a third partner. So now, it's more important than ever that I work here. It's my baby. Plus, I've gotten to know the regulars and I love getting to know new people.

In the corner of my eye, I see Mack with her new girlfriend, Stacy. It took us some time, but we were able to get over our breakup and, in true lesbian fashion, became good friends. Still, I see her look at me sometimes and I know her mind takes her places that go beyond friendship. There's nothing I can do about it. Mack knows where I stand.

Surprisingly, Amelia and Mack get on well now, too. It was awkward as hell when we first started hanging out together again. But Amelia soon put Mack at ease. It's her superpower. She laughs when I say that.

Stacy is just another number in a long line of women Mack has dated over the past two years. It may sound egotistical, but I hope she isn't waiting for me to become single again. Of course, she doesn't know that Amelia and I are mated. I once floated the idea of bringing Mack into the fold regarding Amelia's true lineage.

In the end, we discussed it with the entire Loch family. It was agreed that Mack should stay in the dark. There is still a consensus that the existence of vampires should remain a secret to the human population. Although, from what Amelia has told me, Mohan, the Grand Master, is coming up against more opposition. A group has formed that wishes for vampires to be revealed. I wonder if Harlan and Victoria are a part of it?

Now that we've started to plan the wedding, I need to tell my parents. It's non-negotiable in my mind. My worry is that Amelia will feel differently. What happens if Mohan forbids me? If I present him with a *fait accompli*, what would happen? No, I couldn't go behind Amelia's back.

Speaking of the very sexy devil. I sense her over at the other side of the club. She must have entered through the back. My eyes instantly scan the ocean of bodies dancing. Chuckling, I watch several women openly ogle my fiancée. I laugh because Amelia won't have noticed the attention she is receiving as her eyes will be firmly on mine.

The crowd parts, and she glides through the throng of people. Her eyes sparkle under the strobe lights. Oh momma, she's wearing her black and purple bodice with skin-tight black jeans and sinfully delicious high heels. Her hair is tied up in a high ponytail. If the bar wasn't so busy, I would take her to the office and strip her naked.

The smirk plastered on her gorgeous face tells me she is happy with the effect she's having over me.

"Hello, my love." She purrs.

The music is loud, but I hear her clearly. I wonder how that works. As well as hearing her in my mind, it's like I

25

can tune the world out and pinpoint her voice. Everything around me falls silent. Is that another ability unique only to a few vampires?

"That's quite the outfit, Ms. Loch."

"This old thing," she teases.

We smile stupidly at each other. Amelia leans over, taking my face in her hands. Her eyes feel as if they are staring into my soul. "I love you."

The kiss she gives me almost has my knees buckling.

"Mmm, I love you too." Inhaling her mouth one more time, I finally pull myself away and continue working.

Kit shakes her head, laughing as I pass her. "You two are so fucking hot."

I smile because she's not wrong.

"Hi, what can I get you?" The guy is a typical frat bro. Not our usual clientele, but we try to welcome everyone.

"How about a night with you and that piece of fine ass you were kissing?"

I know he's drunk, and maybe he wouldn't normally be such a douche, but I haven't got the patience to deal with his bullshit. Shaking my head, I signal Garrett.

The drunk asshole leans over, his hand shoots out to stop me from leaving. My eyes stare daggers, but he doesn't notice because he's too busy crumbling to the floor. Amelia has his hand in hers. By the pained look on the guy's face, she is crushing his metacarpals.

"I think it's time you left. Take your friends with you," she practically growls.

Stepping back, Amelia lets go of his hand. The dumbass tries to save face in front of his friends. His lunge is halted by Garrett's tree-sized hands clamping over his shoulder.

Amelia steps forward into the guy's space. Leaning in, she whispers something in his ear that makes him blanch. I don't want to know what she said.

Amelia is generally a calm person, but if she feels anyone is a threat to me, a very different side to her surfaces.

The people at the bar who witnessed the altercation cheer as the frat boys are removed.

"Take a break, my love." Amelia isn't asking. She wants to make sure I'm okay.

Confirming Kit has everything under control, I go to the office with Amelia. The moment the door closes, she has me in her arms.

"Are you okay?"

I breathe her in, just because I can. "I'm perfectly fine. I could have handled him, honey."

"You shouldn't have to. I'm going to ask the bouncers to be more stringent with who they let in."

"Darling, you can't know who's going to turn out to be an asshole. Alcohol makes people stupid. Trust that I can look after myself. I did for a long time before we met." Smiling, I tug her pouting bottom lip with my teeth. "Kiss me."

The kiss turns heated instantly. I should get back to the bar, but Amelia is addictive. I can't get enough of her kisses, of her body. My butt hits the desk with a thud. The sound of multiple things falling and banging on the office floor momentarily distracts us. But it is only a brief second. Amelia's lips are back on my body. A wanting moan echoes through the office as I give myself to her completely. Amelia relieves me of my jeans and panties. I'll give it to her, she's efficient.

Wrapping my legs around her waist, I scoot back on the desk. "Inside," I pant. Amelia is more than happy to comply. Her deft fingers take a quick swipe through my excitement before thrusting inside. This is quick and dirty, and I love it.

The thumping bass covers my scream as I come.

"Holy shit." My legs are still gripping Amelia's body. "My god, you're good at that."

"Do you want to talk about it?" Her question catches me off guard.

Talk about what?

"You want to tell your parents. About me."

I should have realized she'd read my thoughts.

"You really want to talk about it right now, babe? I'm half-naked in the office and you're still inside me."

Kissing me, she takes a step back, forcing me to unwrap myself. I feel the loss of her body keenly.

"Erin, your anxiety is palpable. I don't want you to keep things from me. We talk about everything, even if you think I might get upset."

"I have no worries about that. I'm... I don't know. I'm worried about the consequences. What if Mohan gets upset, or what if my parents freak out and start telling people?"

"Before we met," Amelia begins, handing me my clothes. "I would never have entertained telling a human about myself. The thought terrified me, if I'm honest."

"But you *did* tell a human."

"Yes, because I could trust you. I knew you were safe, and, frankly, I had no choice once my soul found yours."

"But I do have a choice. I could keep quiet and hope they don't notice that I never age."

"Is that what you truly want?"

"No."

"Then you tell them. Do you want to take it to Mohan first?"

"Yes, I think that's wise. This doesn't just affect me. I would never forgive myself if anyone got hurt because of me."

"You really think your parents will react so badly?"

"Who knows? I hope not, but as you said, humans have been brought up on lies about your species. That's going to be difficult to overcome."

Amelia takes me in her arms. "I have faith, my love. Let's call on Mohan tomorrow."

"What if they disown me?"

That's what has really been weighing on me. I know my parents love me unconditionally, but this is a big ask, right? I'm literally going to change. Sure, I'll still look the same and my personality will be that of their daughter, but the fact remains, I will be different. My life is already so ensconced in Amelia's world, I feel myself drifting farther away from what I now consider my old life.

"I find it hard to believe that will happen. But if it does, you have me and my family. Hell, Erin, you have my entire species at your back. You are loved. It will hurt. There is no denying that, but you will survive and we will move forward."

"Thank you." I bury my head in her neck, needing her comfort. "I should get back to work."

"Don't stay late. I'll wait up."

The last thing I want to do is go back to serving drunk patrons. The sex and emotional toll of our conversation has left me feeling raw. Straightening my clothes, I head back out. Amelia is already halfway across the club, heading for the secret stairs that lead to our penthouse apartment. Kit gives me a knowing smirk. My face must still be flushed.

Mack is leaning at the other end of the bar. Stacy is chatting away, but Mack is looking at me.

Waving, I make my way over. "Hey, it's been a minute."

"The hospital is understaffed as per usual. I've been catching double shifts for a couple of weeks."

"Well, it's good to see you. Need another?"

"Sure, why not? I've got the day off tomorrow."

I set about pouring Mack's favorite IPA.

She leans closer. "Want to grab a coffee tomorrow?"

"Sure. Can I call you? I've got something I need to take care of, and I'm not sure how long that will take."

"No worries. I look forward to it."

Stacy is giving me the evil eye and Mack either doesn't care or is ignoring her.

Smiling Mack's way one last time, I take a step away. "Okay, well, I should get back to it."

The evening passes in a blur. I avoid having another conversation with Mack. All I want to do is soak in the tub with Amelia and a glass of wine. Maybe some chocolate.

As soon as the bar is wiped down and the door is locked, I sprint up to the apartment. The smell of roses hits me first, then the candlelight.

"In here, my love."

I follow Amelia's melodic voice to the ensuite.

"I thought you might need a soak." She continues.

"Did you read my mind, Ms. Loch?" I can't stop a smile from forming.

"Actually, I didn't. The club was insane. I thought you'd need to unwind."

"Will you join me?"

"My pleasure."

Tomorrow is still causing me a little anxiety. But as I lay wrapped in Amelia's arms, I know it will be alright. No matter what happens.

Four

I wake with a start, my breathing labored. The dream is still swimming in my subconscious. There's a film of sweat on my brow and upper lip. Amelia is sleeping soundly beside me, completely unaware of the turmoil raging through my body.

Closing my eyes tight, I will the dream away. But the more I try, the clearer it becomes. We were making love by the ocean. Clear blue skies as far as the eye could see. I can still feel the pure ecstasy of Amelia's touch. But then, clouds rolled in. Something inside me turned the pleasure into terror as a hunger built. A hunger for Amelia's blood. I was bloodthirsty. I sought her neck, roughly taking her head in my hands. I was relentless in my pursuit of biting her. Even now, my mouth is watering at the thought of gorging on Amelia's life force. The moment my teeth pierced her neck, I woke up.

It was just a dream, right? If that's true, why does it feel like something wrong is happening inside me? Panic washes over me.

"Morning, my love." Amelia's sleep-riddled voice rips me from my worries.

"Morning," I stammer.

Do I want her to know about the dream?

"Are you alright?" Amelia pulls me into her warm body. She wraps an arm around me and buries her head in my hair.

"Fine, sweetheart. Just a nightmare." My heart is hammering in my chest as my mouth comes into contact with her skin. What the hell is wrong with me?

"Oh no, let me kiss you better." I'm thankful that Amelia's mind is focused elsewhere. It wouldn't take much for her to read my mind. Although, I'm not sure if a dream can be classed as conscious thought.

As she assaults my jaw with her divine kisses, I feel a mental barrier drop, shielding my mind. The action must alert Amelia, because she abruptly stops kissing me. Her eyes level with mine and I see the concern. "What's going on?"

"Wow, your mom was right. This thing is developing."

My attempt at humor falls flat.

"Erin?"

"It was just a bad dream."

"Then why are you blocking me? What is it you don't want me to see?"

Closing my eyes, I try to calm my thoughts. There is no reason to blow this out of proportion. As my mind calms, the barrier fades, and I feel our connection once more.

Amelia's brow furrows as I recall my nightmare. The mere memory is still causing discomfort. Can she feel that too?

"You're worried this means something?"

I can always count on Amelia to grasp the seriousness of a situation. Most people would brush something like this off, but if we've learned one thing together, it's that our situation is unique.

Barty is the only other known vampire to have mated successfully with a human. After our time with him and Anya in Ireland, we learned a little more, but nothing that gave us solid answers. We discovered that both of us, Anya and I, ingested our partner's blood pre-mating, therefore somehow allowing for the bond to take. Anya never mentioned feeling bloodlust, though.

"Call Anya and ask."

"What if she's never felt it?"

"Then we seek council from Mohan. This could be just a nightmare. You've been under tremendous pressure for the past two years. This year is especially hard for us both."

"No more than usual."

"Waiting can be the hardest thing to endure. Trust me, I know. I had to wait twenty-nine years for you."

"Wow, that was cheesy!" I burst out laughing at Amelia's crestfallen face. She's too cute sometimes. "I love cheesy, and I love you."

We embrace tightly. Maybe we can restart the day by acting out the first part of my dream? Amelia's wandering hands make me smile.

"Do you want me to grab our toy?" she asks.

"No, I need your fingers."

My legs part instantly. I welcome her weight on me and her bare skin against mine. Our sex life has changed somewhat over the last two years. Our bond becomes stronger when we make love. Sure, we still enjoy a quickie now and then. A passion-filled fuck always does the trick too, but nothing brings us together more than when we take our time.

Amelia's hair hangs down, shielding us from everything. Our eyes lock and then something happens that I can't explain. The blue and gold lights that encompass us as we climax appear, but they aren't surrounding us this time. I see them shining brightly in Amelia's eyes.

Pictures form in my head. I'm witnessing Amelia's life through her own eyes. We haven't even touched each other yet.

"Erin?" she whispers. "What's happening?"

"I can see your memories."

"I think I can see yours."

We stay silent, allowing whatever is unfolding. A sudden urge to kiss her overcomes my senses, and I take her forcefully. Our lips collide repeatedly. My hands tug at her hair. It feels as if my entire body is amped up with adrenaline.

Rolling her over, I plunge my fingers inside. The urgency isn't abating. Amelia mirrors my actions. The moment she enters me, my vision goes black.

A heavy fog fills my mind. My body feels heavy. Am I shaking?

"Erin?"

"What, what happened?"

Finally, Amelia's blurred outline triggers my brain into action. I sit up with panic filling my chest. I can't remember what happened after everything went black.

"It's okay, you're okay. Just breathe, my love."

My eyes focus on Amelia's, grounding me once more. "Amelia, what the hell was that?"

"I don't know."

"Did you pass out?"

"No, but I saw everything you saw. Your mind went dark, and then there were images of people. I didn't recognize any of them."

"Images of people?"

"You don't remember?"

"No, everything went black, and that's it."

"We need to call Mohan and the doctor."

"Why does this always happen when we're having sex?"

Amelia laughs. "Because it's when we are closest."

"It's inconvenient." I chuckle.

"You're telling me."

Our levity keeps us from freaking out. Another thing we've learned over the past two years. Laugh, because the alternative sucks.

∞

Hushed voices greet us as we enter the Loch main residence. It might be Victoria and Harlan's home, but I see it as the Loch family HQ. It's where you'll find everyone if something is going on. And, by the look on everyone's face, something is definitely going on.

"What's wrong?" Amelia cuts to the chase.

"A Fallen has escaped," Harlan answers.

"How is that even possible?"

As far as I'm aware, Mohan knows of all the Fallen vampires. Thankfully, they aren't a regular occurrence, but they exist. Poor vampires who were unable to mate before their thirtieth birthday. From what I've been told, the Grand Master has knowledge of all the vampires in his domain.

When they identify a Fallen, they take them away for the safety of humankind. Unfortunately, I know there is no cure for their madness. Doctor Mendhi has been working nonstop to find something that will help. So far, he's had no luck. All Fallen vampires go to a secure location, where the doctor tries different treatments.

"Mohan has sent an alert out," Laurence adds.

"What can we do?" Amelia asks.

"Be on the lookout," Marcus says. The family is clearly worried. This is the first time I've faced anything like this. The Lochs, like all other vampire families, are no different from humans, really. Except that vampires have the Fallen. Bloodthirsty monsters. Every human is in danger now.

"We should close the club," I whisper to Amelia. It would be a meat market for a Fallen vampire.

"Yes, you're right. I'll make some calls." Amelia leaves to call Claire, I presume.

Suddenly, I'm terrified. "I need to call my parents."

"Invite them here. I think it's time they knew the truth." Victoria draws me into a hug.

Understandably, my parents are a little taken aback at my request. Especially when I told them to pack a bag. I've decided the best way to tell them is the same way Amelia told me. Let the evidence speak for me.

Victoria and Harlan are in the living room with the rest of the family as I gather up all the documents. Of course, they offered to help, but I needed a few minutes to ready myself. Amelia argued with me until Lucille took her roughly by the arm. That shifted the argument from me to her, allowing me to slip out of the room.

The worst-case scenario has set up residence in my brain. I know I have Amelia and the rest of the Lochs by my side, but the thought of losing my parents causes a searing pain in my chest.

The doorbell rings, echoing through the Loch mansion. My parents have been here many times before, but this feels like the first time. Soon, they will know the truth and will see everything anew. God, I hope they understand.

The Lochs and my parents are embracing as I come down the staircase with my arms laden with documents, pictures, and ancient texts. I've studied all of them in depth. Even after accepting that vampires existed, I continued to read. It's all quite fascinating.

"Erin, honey. What on earth is going on?"

"Come into the living room, Mom, and I'll explain everything."

The ten Lochs cram themselves onto one sofa. I ask Amelia to sit with her family. I need to do this alone. My parents sit calmly, but I can see they're worried.

"I need to tell you something, and it's not going to sound very believable."

"Erin?"

"Please, Dad, just listen."

He nods and falls silent. I lay out the books and scrolls on the floor, facing them.

"I need you both to read through these. Once you have, you'll understand, and I'll answer any questions."

"Sweetie—"

"Please, just read."

My hands form tight fists as my parents pick up a book each and begin reading. The room is silent, but I hear Amelia loud and clear. She's doing her very best to keep me calm.

Now and then my mother raises her eyebrow at something written. My father is harder to gauge. They continue reading for what seems like hours.

Gently, my mom closes the book in her lap and looks up. Her eyes convey uncertainty, as if she can't decide if the words she's just read can be believed.

"E-erin, you're trying to tell us that...that—"

"Vampires exist." I finish for her. My father rushes to his feet and paces the floor, his eyes on the Loch family.

"You can't be serious." Mom laughs. But I see it in her eyes. She knows it's true.

"It's true," Amelia voices confidently.

Silence descends again. I'm at a total loss for what to do next. I don't want them running out scared, especially now, with a Fallen on the loose.

"But...vampires are evil," Mom whispers. I feel Amelia's eye roll before I see it.

"No, they're not. I promise you. Mom, Dad, everything you've been told about them is a fabrication."

Mom scratches her head, her eyes downcast. My father is still pacing and then he's still. His eyes train on the Lochs.

"Will you hurt Erin? I mean, do you drink her blood?"

I want to laugh at how ludicrous he sounds, but then I stop and recall how I thought about those kinds of things before I knew any better.

"No. We don't drink human blood. Only animal," Harlan answers.

"Is that by choice or—"

"We aren't made to hurt humans, Robert. The taste of human blood is quite repulsive. We aren't mythical creatures. We evolved, just as humans did."

43

"And you knew this before being with Amelia?" Dad is looking at me now, and I still can't get a read on his thoughts.

"Amelia told me early on. There is a lot to explain, but for now, I just need you to process this. I'm not in danger from them. Neither are you nor any other human."

"That's not strictly true," Lucille pipes up. I cast her a glare that she rolls her eyes at. "Tell them everything."

Five

Mom and Dad asked for a little space after Harlan and Victoria filled them in on the Fallen, and how one had escaped custody. I was almost hopeful they would accept everything they'd learned up until then.

My mom grew quiet and pale with every second that passed. Dad continued pacing frantically. I could feel Amelia in the periphery of my mind desperately trying to calm my raging anxiety, but she had little success.

They rattled through questions, which Victoria answered honestly. Ones I hadn't thought to ask myself. Such as the survival rate of humans after being attacked by a Fallen. The answer was bone chilling: none survived. The sheer blood lust meant a Fallen drank the human dry.

Victoria went on to explain that most fatalities were covered up by vampires in the police and government. Thankfully, attacks were rare nowadays, due to Mohan's leadership and tight surveillance of vampires approaching mating age.

According to their history, though, it hadn't been as easy as it was now. Until this moment, I never fully understood the difficulties vampires faced throughout time. Not only were they hiding their true selves, they had to find solutions to deal with the Fallen.

Harlan looked somber as he took over from Victoria. He went on to explain how the Fallen almost ripped apart the vampire community. There were those who wished to cull vampires who hadn't mated twenty-four hours before their thirtieth birthday. The other half wanted to try to care for the lost souls. Hiding them in institutes or the equivalent of that time period.

There were uprisings and revolts. Countless deaths as they fought over a way to suppress the Fallen in a way that appeased everyone. That's when Mohan became the beacon of light the community still stood by. He took charge, using humanity's superstition to cover disappearances and deaths. The Salem Witch Trials were not all they seemed to be.

Tragically, the women who died by fire and drowning were necessary sacrifices. The trials gave Mohan and his team time to get the Fallen under some sort of control.

This history added such a layer of weight to the already overloaded minds of my parents that I really couldn't blame them for needing space.

They've been upstairs for hours now and I'm lost. All I want to do is hug them and tell them everything is okay. They have no need to worry, but that would be a lie.

I'm worried. An escaped Fallen vampire is no small thing. People will die. Innocent people, and there is nothing I can do. It's times like this I wish I'd already changed. If I had a little more strength and speed, I would be useful instead of a liability. As is, I have to wait around while Amelia and the rest of her family help Mohan come up with a plan.

Every vampire in the city is on high alert. I've never seen the Grand Master looking so stricken. The council arrived at the Loch mansion an hour ago. Amelia gave me a kiss before shutting herself away in her father's study with the rest of the guests.

If I walk around this house one more time, I'm going to go nuts. I can't take the silence anymore. My parents have to talk to me, whether or not they like it.

Storming up the stairs, I take a breath before entering their room. Mom is lying on the bed staring at the ceiling, and Dad is still fucking pacing.

"You have to talk to me."

Mom sits up wide-eyed. Dad finally stills. "This is a lot, Erin."

Dad is stating the obvious, and that's fine, as long as they speak.

"It is, and I'm sorry. I've struggled with this for a long time. Telling you wasn't a decision I came to lightly, but with everything going on, I needed you to understand and be safe."

"Vampires, Erin!"

Okay, so Mom isn't processing all that well.

"Yes, vampires. But not the ones we've learned about in fantasy movies or books. They're just people, like you and me."

"Not quite, love," Dad scoffs.

"Dad. They *are* like us. They drink blood like we drink water. It sustains them. They have jobs, families, and pay their taxes."

"We're worried, sweetie. Worried about what this means for you." Mom slips off the bed and stands by Dad.

"You expect us to be okay with you changing into one of them? We'd be losing our little girl."

"No, you won't. I'll still be me, just a little different. Guys, Amelia is everything to me. She is my life. I cannot even imagine a time where I'm not with her. That's what it means to be bonded. We can read each other's thoughts. I can sense her presence everywhere. What we have is special, and I'd change into a vampire a thousand times over if that's what it took to be with her for eternity. I can't ask you to fully understand, but I can ask you to trust me. Please?"

"Erin, we're pretty open-minded people. Just give us some time, okay?" Dad steps forward and hugs me. That's all I need for now. I'll give them the space they need, as long as they stay close.

"You still need to stay here. Until the Fallen is recaptured."

Both look uneasy with the demand, but it's tough and they know it.

"If you feel that uncomfortable around everyone, I'm sure I can arrange for you to have food delivered to your room."

"No. Victoria and Harlan have been kind enough to open their home to us. We'll dine with everyone. There might be some questions, if that's okay?"

"Ask anything and of anyone. I love you."

Mom sobs, which breaks my heart. I never wanted to hurt or worry them. Downstairs, I hear voices. Amelia's voice rings clearly through my mind. They have a plan.

Kissing my parents, I leave them to their thoughts. Right now I need to be with my other family, helping wherever possible.

"Hey, how did it go?" I ask Amelia. She's standing on the outskirts of the room, watching everyone.

"Well. Mohan has it under control. So far, there is no sign of the Fallen, but it won't stay that way for long. The thirst will be unbearable by now and unfortunately, the best way for us to get a lead on them is to wait until someone is attacked."

"God, that's awful."

Amelia nods. "I'm surprised it hasn't already happened."

"Will Mohan and the council stay close by?"

"Yes. Mohan is staying in one of our guest rooms. We think it's wise to keep the council separate. If anything happens, we need to keep the chain of command safe."

"You think the Fallen would attack the council?"

"It's just a precaution. When the vampire is located, it will be all hands on deck to bring them in. Things could go wrong."

"Amelia—"

"I have to help them, Erin. It's my duty to keep people safe, as much as it's the Grand Master's."

Suddenly, Mohan makes a break for the door. "We have a reported attack. Let's go."

Amelia kisses me quickly on the cheek. I hear her tell me to stay put, which pisses me off somewhat.

The house grows quiet again, and it makes me restless. Grabbing my coat, I head for the garden. I'm not stupid enough to go after Amelia and the council. They are the experts, and I'm just human. A brisk walk around the grounds should help burn some of my frustrations away. I hope.

Only yesterday, Amelia and I were lost in our own little world, dreaming of our upcoming nuptials. How I wish we could go back to that. Instead of wishing for things that are impossible, I focus on Amelia's thoughts. She's calm, which is good. I can feel her nerves and adrenaline. Our connection is definitely stronger.

My feet take me automatically around the house. I enjoy walking this way when we visit because the view of the rose gardens is quite breathtaking. A stone catches my foot and I stumble. As I fall, I feel a burning at the back of my throat. It's the same sensation I had in my dream. One of ravenous hunger.

I've fallen to my knees, my palms face down on the gravel path. I can smell my own ferrous blood from the scrapes I must have sustained. My mouth waters and my vision blurs. I can sense someone. It's not Amelia. Turning my head, I come face to face with a young woman. Her eyes are a dark shade of red, almost black. Her body is shaking as she grips the stone bench in front of her. Our eyes remain locked. I can hear her plea for help. I can feel the pain in her throat.

Standing, I face her fully. I'm not scared, which maybe is a mistake. There is no doubt she is the Fallen vampire everyone is looking for. What I don't understand is what she wants from me. Shouldn't she be attacking me, consumed with insanity and bloodlust?

"What do you need?" I hear myself speaking, but it's as if I'm no longer in control of my body.

"Help me," she pleads.

Help her. Yes, that's what I must do, I feel it viscerally in my chest. I focus on her mind, blocking out everything else. Her thoughts are consumed with pain and darkness.

Walking to her, I ready myself for what's to come. I know how to help. Exposing my neck, I take the woman by the head and lower her mouth.

"Take what you need."

Her teeth pierce my skin, but it doesn't hurt. My mind is completely shrouded by hers. The darkness abates as she drinks from me. Hands grip my hips as she takes what she needs. A wave of...not pain, but not entirely pleasure either...rolls over me. A comfort, perhaps? It feels almost intimate. Like she is seeing me profoundly, truly. A way that feels familiar. A way that only Amelia has experienced.

And then she is gone. As if it were a dream, I come to my senses. I'm standing by the bench, my mind foggy. Did that really happen? Reaching for my neck, I feel for puncture wounds. There are none. Am I losing my mind?

Car tires screeching to a stop pulls me back to reality. Amelia is screaming my name over and over. Something must have happened. I race to the house, only to find everyone searching rooms calling for me.

"Amelia, what's happened?"

My voice calls to her like a siren. Amelia pushes through the crowd, taking me in her arms.

"Are you okay?"

She doesn't give me time to answer. Her hands roam my head, neck, and body. Her eyes are frantic, and I know she is experiencing sheer panic.

"Amelia, my love, I'm fine. I was in the garden."

"You disappeared from my mind. As if you no longer existed. I've never been so scared in my life."

Pulling me in again, Amelia sobs into my hair.

"I'm here. It's okay."

I go to break away, but she holds me tighter. More arms surround me and I see the Loch family joining in the embrace. They were all terrified. I can see it on each of their faces.

"Erin?" My mom is calling me from the top of the stairs. I can only imagine how weird this looks.

"Guys, I need to breathe." My little quip earns me a chuckle. Everyone steps back apart from Amelia, who I'm afraid won't ever let me go. "Baby, I'm okay. You need to let go."

"I can't," she whispers. I've never seen her so shaken.

"Amelia," Victoria says softly into her daughter's ear. "She's safe, honey. Let her go."

A few moments pass, but eventually Amelia straightens, her eyes boring into mine. I feel our connection. I hear her pouring her love into me. Reaching for her face, I pull her down for a long, deep kiss. It might not ease her fear entirely, but it helps. I can feel her relax a little.

"Did you find them?" I ask the room.

"No. The attack report was false," Lucas answers.

"So nobody got hurt?"

"Not this time," Mohan replies.

"May I examine you?" Dr. Mendhi asks.

"Yes, if you must. I'm alright, though. I was just in the garden."

The doctor takes me to Harlan's office. He mutters to himself and jots notes in a small notepad. Instead of worry, I sense something else. Is it...excitement? The incongruity is unnerving. Amelia follows close behind.

"Did you feel our connection break?" she asks.

"I don't know."

My answer is honest. I can't say with certainty that I know what the hell happened. Truthfully, I fear the answer. Why would I offer myself up to a Fallen vampire? And why didn't it rip me to shreds?

"I've got a headache."

The doctor completes his exam quickly. There is nothing out of the ordinary, but I find his questions invasive. His frustration at my lack of answers is palpable.

It's a side of him I've never seen before. All I want is to be alone with Amelia. I'm having to keep her mind at bay until Dr. Mendhi leaves.

The moment he leaves us alone, I allow Amelia in fully. Her face pales when she hears my thoughts.

"It can't have happened, right?" I need Amelia to tell me what the fuck is going on.

"I—" Amelia Loch is rarely at a loss for words.

"Amelia, tell me I'm not going out of my mind. Did I really allow a vampire to bite me?"

She swallows several times. "Yes. I saw it in your mind. It doesn't feel like a false memory."

Her words pierce through my defenses, and I crumble to the floor. I must have cried out loud because my mother comes crashing through the door. Amelia hasn't moved. Mom cradles me in her arms as I cry.

None of this makes any sense. Despite offering myself up to this woman, I still feel violated. I see her blood-red eyes in my mind and I know Amelia is hurting. I've allowed another vampire to put their lips on me. And yet, even though I know it's wrong, I have this uncontrollable urge to feel that closeness again. To feel the Fallen.

I want to scream and shout, but a surge of heat in my throat steals my breath. It's happening again. I can feel the thirst taking over. Pushing my mother, I scramble away from her. I know I'd never hurt her, but right now, I'm not me!

Six

"Erin? Sweetie, what's wrong?"

My mom looks hurt that I pushed her away, but there's no time to explain. Amelia steps forward, taking her by the arm, gently leading her outside. If Mom protests, I don't hear her.

My throat is still on fire, and my mind is becoming foggy. Blackness is creeping in once more. Is she back? The woman with the red eyes. A warmth on my cheek pulls me temporarily from my nightmare.

"My love. Tell me what you are feeling."

"Blackness," is all I can say.

"I can't feel you anymore, Erin. I need you to tell me everything you see."

"It's just black. My throat…" I feel my hand wrap around my throat as if that would help stave off the hunger. "I need to drink, Amelia."

She looks at me with an understanding I can't fully process. "Here, take this."

A cold steel flask is placed in my other hand. Without question, I raise it to my lips and drink greedily. The thick liquid coats my mouth, sliding down my throat with ease. I feel the temporary relief but it's fleeting. I've just had my first real taste of Red. Gone is the metallic tang. It's as if I've swallowed nothing more than water. What does this mean?

"I need…" What is it I need? I need to find the source of this hunger. I'm aware enough to know this isn't me, it's someone, something else. Staggering to my feet, I grip Amelia tightly. "Amelia, I need to find her."

"Find who?"

"The woman with the red eyes, the one who fed on me."

I feel Amelia tense and I know she's doing everything in her power to remain calm. Does she feel betrayed? I would if things were reversed.

"Why do you need to find her?"

"Because she's the reason I'm thirsty."

I wish I could explain better, but that would mean I understand what the hell is going on myself.

"Help me, please."

"We need to tell Mohan."

I want to protest. If this woman is the Fallen vampire everyone is looking for, they won't hesitate to kill her when she is found. I can't let that happen. I know there is a reason she found me, fed on me.

"No, not yet. Please, Amelia."

"Erin, he must know. We need help. You need help."

Reluctantly I agree. It's not as if I can find her by myself. And even if I could, I have no clue what I'm walking into. Earlier in the garden could have been a fluke. The woman may just rip my throat out the next time she sees me.

Amelia helps me into a wingback chair before leaving the room. I take in the quiet solace for a moment, trying desperately to gather my thoughts. The Red I drank minutes ago is still helping, albeit on a small level. The hunger is sated enough that I can think.

I need to understand how I'm linked to the Fallen. Why had she sought me out, and what happened to her when she drank from me? Amelia steps in moments later with Mohan, Harland, Victoria, and my parents.

"Erin, dear. How are you feeling?" Mohan is a softly spoken man. I adore him. Amelia is right. If we're to figure out what is happening to me, he is the one to trust.

"She's close, Mohan."

"Who?"

"The Fallen. She's close and she needs my help." I see them all exchange a worried look. "I know it sounds crazy, but I can feel her in here." Poking my head, I shoot Amelia an imploring look. She must understand. I don't want another vampire in my head—ever—but I can't do a thing to control it.

"Harlan, call the doctor in, please." Harlan leaves immediately. "Erin, can you tell us what happened? Everything you can remember."

"I had a nightmare."

It makes sense now. The reason I dreamed of biting Amelia. The Fallen must have already escaped and been on her way to me. We're linked somehow.

"I felt bloodlust toward Amelia. It was unlike anything I've ever experienced. We just thought it was a dream, nothing more."

"Our connection has been getting stronger," Amelia adds. "We intended to speak to you today, before we found out about the Fallen."

"When you all left to follow up on the reported attack, I needed some air. Walking around the gardens, I felt that hunger again, and then... I felt her. She was leaning by the bench."

"Did she attack you?" Dad asks. All eyes are on me with rapt attention.

"No. She asked me for help. And I just knew what I had to do. I let her feed from me."

Their gasps are audible.

"She drank and then left. My connection to her was severed, and then you all came back."

"Dr. Mendhi? Have you any idea what this means?" Mohan is all business now.

"I'll need to do some tests. Erin, do you feel the connection to her now?"

I shake my head. "Not like before. I can't feel her, but I have the hunger again. My throat is burning."

There is a commotion by the office door. A man I've never met before whispers something in Mohan's ear. His eyes widen before he schools his features once more.

"Another Fallen has escaped."

The room is deathly silent now, with all eyes once again on me.

"You need to get her somewhere safe," Amelia growls at Mohan.

"Yes, indeed. Gather your things. We will go to my house."

Which one, I want to ask. Mohan has property all over the world. The second thing I want to do is protest. There is no point in hiding. They will find me. I can feel it. They are driven to seek me out, just as they are driven to consume human blood.

Amelia must sense my hesitation, which means our connection is still there, even if it's tentative.

"We are *going*, Erin." She leaves no room for argument.

"Now, wait just a minute." My mother is red-faced and angry. "No one is taking my daughter anywhere until you explain what the hell is going on. Hours ago, you told us she was safe. Your kind would never hurt her and yet here she is telling us someone has fed from her!"

Amelia's body is shaking as she tries to keep calm. All she wants to do is scoop me up and run away to a place where I will be secure. Her patience for talking is running out fast, but out of respect for me and my parents, she's trying not to blow.

"Erin would never be harmed by one of us. I can't explain what's going on. Whatever is happening to Erin has never occurred before. We are all at a loss, and we need time to figure it out, but Erin needs to be somewhere safe for us to do that."

"She's coming home with us," my mom seethes.

"No, Mom." The situation needs to be de-escalated, and fast. "I need to go with Mohan. And you need to come too."

"Erin, this isn't up for discussion, young lady."

"No. It's not," I agree with my father. "I'm a grown woman and have made my decision."

"Then, we shall make ours. We can't support this, Erin. You should be with someone human, someone who isn't going to put you in danger."

Hurt flashes across Amelia's face and slices through my chest.

"If you follow these lunatics, you do so without our blessing."

"Please don't say something you can't take back," Victoria says. Her voice is like steel. She makes a show of coming to my side and resting her hand on my shoulder. "Erin is your daughter. She's our daughter, too. We will do everything to protect her."

"Erin?" I look at my mom. She has unshed tears pooling in her eyes. "Please, baby. Come home with us."

"I am home. Mom, there are things in the human world that are just as likely to cause me pain. We can't control everything. Amelia is my soulmate. I'll never leave her."

"Then you've made your decision." I have never heard my dad sound so cold. "I hope you know what you're doing."

Without another word or glance toward me, he ushers my sobbing mother from the room.

Tears come instantly. My body shudders with grief. My worst nightmare is coming true. I've just lost my parents. Amelia's arms engulf me, and I cling to her like a life raft.

"They're just reacting. I promise you they'll be back."

"We need to go, Amelia," Mohan says softly. Amelia lifts me effortlessly into her arms.

"Ask Lucille to pack a bag for us, please."

I've learned that, as much as Amelia and Lucille come to blows, in a crisis, they are the two siblings most likely to band together.

The Red is wearing off and I can feel my mind fighting to keep the link with Amelia.

"Drink," I gasp after a strong surge rips through my throat. I grit my teeth, trying hard not to think about Amelia's neck, which is so close to my lips.

"Red," Amelia barks. She sets me down gently, handing me the flask given to her by Marcus. The siblings are unaware of what has occurred, which is why he is staring at me wide-eyed as I drink.

"Amelia?"

"Not now, Marcus. Later. We'll explain everything."

As before, the Red helps. Only moments pass before Amelia is on the move again. I curl into her body, needing her warmth and strength. A motorcade is waiting for us outside. If this wasn't so serious, I'd probably laugh.

Bundled into the back of an SUV—which I'm sure is armored—I lay my head against Amelia's shoulder. She's still holding me tight. Whether that's for my benefit or hers, I'm not sure.

As we travel further away from the Loch mansion, the hunger all but disappears. My mind feels lighter, I feel in control again. Sitting up, I wipe my hands down my face. God knows what I must look like.

"I feel better."

Amelia takes my face in her hands and studies my face. "You *look* better. Our connection is back."

I can feel it too. As strong as ever. "Where are we going?"

"Ireland. We need to talk to Barty. Mohan agrees."

It makes sense for us to seek one of the oldest vampires in existence, especially when he mated with a human successfully, too.

"Surely Anya would have mentioned it if she'd experienced this."

"I believe so, but what other choice do we have? As far as I know, nobody, vampire or human, has ever formed a link with a Fallen. There is also the fact our bond is changing somehow. There are too many questions and not enough answers."

I feel her irritation as if it were my own. "Amelia, we'll figure this out."

"We have to. I can't lose you, Erin. It would destroy me."

The vulnerability and fear I saw earlier in her is back.

"Never. I'll always be here."

It's a promise I shouldn't offer so easily. It's clear that there are many things that could stop us from having an eternity together. But I can't think like that. We have to believe everything will work out as it should.

The SUV comes to a stop forty minutes later. Mohan and the rest of the Loch family are already aboard his private jet.

"I can walk, my love." I grin when Amelia tries to carry me again.

"I just need to hold you close, just a little while longer."

I nod. I can't deny her anything. The siblings are remarkably quiet when we take our seats. I can see Lucille is busting a gut, trying to keep her curiosity at bay. From the stern faces of Harlan and Victoria, I gather they've all been told to keep quiet and not ask questions.

As the plane ascends, I feel a breath on the back of my neck. Turning, I come face to face with Lucille, who has her face wedged between mine and Amelia's seats.

"You are so much more interesting than my sister," she whispers, and I can't help but laugh.

Seven

It's raining heavily when the plane touches down on Irish soil. The weather matches my mood. Gray and turbulent. All I want is to spend my days with the woman I love in peace, but it seems the universe has other plans. There is still an hour on the road to travel until we reach Barty and Anya. I wonder if Amelia would allow us to stop for a pint somewhere. Her glare tells me no. Shame. Alcohol would be welcome right about now.

God, I wish I was behind the bar at Insomnia—not to pilfer the liquor. Just dealing with drunk assholes instead of fighting to keep out an unknown vampire who is constantly trying to invade my brain would be great. Or is it her? Since leaving LA, I can no longer tell if it's the same vampire trying to connect. But who else could it be? Surely it's just a coincidence that another Fallen escaped, right?

I'd hoped the next time we saw Barty and Anya would be at our wedding, celebrating, but it seems we only meet in times of uncertainty and drama. Ugh, I hate being at the center of all this.

The motorcade pulls up to the castle. I still have fond memories of our first visit here. I can't believe it's been almost three years. We should have made more time to visit.

I can't help but smile at the memory which flashes across my mind. Amelia rolls her eyes but smiles, too. I'm thinking of Amelia's reaction when we first drove toward the castle. She was irritated that Barty had been so cliché in his choice of home. A nice Gothic castle for a vampire. I giggle at the thought. Barty and Anya are the absolute opposite of what society would expect a vampire to look like. Barty has less of the "I want to suck your blood" vibe and more of the "should we play a full round of golf followed by drinks at the club" vibe.

Our friends are waiting by the door. No doubt Amelia or one of the other family members called ahead. Actually, it was probably Mohan. He has grown close to Barty and Anya over the years. I wonder if they know the full scale of our problem. I say our problem, because no matter what, Amelia is in this with me.

Barty hasn't changed one bit. He still looks like a yuppy. Anya, on the other hand, has cut her hair short and dyed it blonde. She looks amazing.

"Anya, my word, you look stunning."

"Erin, stop. You'll make me blush!" We share a long, tight hug. It's nice to be back. Anya understands what it's been like for me.

"Amelia, Erin, welcome back," Barty booms, smiling from ear to ear. He's usually in a cheerful mood, and it seems today is no different.

"Barty, Anya." Amelia shares a hug with them both.

"So, is it down to business or a drink first?"

"Busine—"

"Drink." Giving Amelia *the look*, I follow Anya through to the living room. It's one thing denying me a pint of beer, quite another denying me a drink at all. I think I deserve it. Hell, we all deserve a few. The roaring fire opposite Barty and Anya's sofa makes me feel instantly at home.

"Don't worry, Amelia, we won't go as heavy on the whiskey as last time."

Last time, I couldn't believe either of them still had a liver!

"Could I have wine instead of whiskey, please?" Anya has an exquisite wine collection.

"I've already poured one for us." Anya winks. "Amelia?"

"Wine, please. I'll leave the whiskey for later."

"How about we get down to business whilst we drink?" Barty reads Amelia's mood well. She doesn't want to socialize. Maybe that's why the rest of the family and Mohan have made themselves scarce. Even Lucille left Amelia alone, which is rare.

We settle down on opposite sofas. Anya and Barty are looking at me expectantly. I don't know where to start. It all sounds completely insane when I go over it in my head.

Sensing my inner struggle, Amelia lays out the facts as we know them. Watching Barty, I can see he's intrigued. Not completely shocked, which is interesting. Anya looks worried, meaning I doubt she ever experienced anything like this.

"Have you encountered anything like this, Barty?" Amelia asks. I'm happy to sit quietly. He strokes his chin, lost in thought. Amelia leans forward, waiting. I take another slug of wine. It's a great vintage.

"There is nothing concrete I can tell you. I need a little time to do research. Mostly, it's myth and legend, but as we all know, there's usually a grain of truth to it."

"To what exactly?" Amelia is growing impatient.

"I don't feel comfortable saying until I know more. I know you're frustrated, Amelia, but please trust me. I'll head up to the library now." He doesn't wait for a reply.

Laying my hand on her thigh, I try to ground her. I know she's scared. What happened at the Loch mansion scared us both, but we have to trust in the people around us.

"How are you now, Erin?" Anya tops up my wine, which is probably a bad idea, but I'm past caring.

"Tired if I'm being honest. Confused and scared, too."

"Understandably."

"I'm sorry we haven't been over to see you. We should have made time."

For whatever reason, it's playing on my mind. Anya and Barty have been great friends and we've neglected that friendship.

"It goes both ways, Erin." She chuckles. "That's the downside to this whole immortality thing. We start to take things for granted. Nothing is urgent and things usually fall by the wayside. Barty and I will arrange a visit. I'd love to see LA again. It's been decades."

"Deal."

"May I borrow one of your motorcycles?" Amelia asks.

Her request isn't a surprise. She's anxious and fidgety. Burning some adrenaline on the back of a bike will do her good. It would for me too, but I already know the answer to that question. It seems I'm going to be under castle-arrest for a little while.

I lean over and kiss her lips. Is that hesitation I feel from her? My heart sinks, but I push it to one side.

"Be safe, my love."

"Always. I'll be back later."

Stalking out of the room with rigid shoulders, Amelia heads for the garage. God, I'd do anything to make her feel better. Anything to take that haunted look from her eyes.

"How's she doing?" Anya is looking at me as I stare after Amelia.

"She's hurt, scared, and a myriad of other things. I don't know what's worse for her. Knowing a Fallen vampire found me or knowing it—sorry, she—fed from me. It's like I cheated on her. I can feel her pain, but she hasn't talked to me. Our bond has grown to the point we can read each other's thoughts, but she's blocking certain things. I haven't pushed. She'll open up when she's ready. I just hope she still feels the same for me."

"There is nothing that could stop her from loving you, Erin."

"Loving and liking are two different things, Anya. She's bound to me. That doesn't mean she has to like it."

"Erin, this is Amelia we're talking about."

"I know. But I betrayed her."

"Did you seek this Fallen vampire? Ask her to feed from you?"

"No, but I told her to when I realized it's what she needed."

"Tell me about that. What you felt."

"As soon as she asked for help, it was like my body went on autopilot. I wasn't scared. I knew she wouldn't kill me. There was a pulsing in my blood. Thinking back, that's what drew me to her. She was calling for it."

"And when she fed?"

"Nothing. It didn't hurt. She took only what she needed and then left."

"Did you see anything?"

"My mind went black. I knew she was bonded to me in some way. That's what alerted Amelia. It seemed our connection broke. I've never seen her so frightened, Anya. She said I vanished from her. She thought I was dead, I'm sure of it."

"In my humble opinion, it's *that* thought which haunts Amelia, not the fact a Fallen bit you."

"Not bit, fed. And I willingly let it happen."

"I'd say willingly is a strong word. There is something happening to you that allowed you to connect to this vampire. Not just any vampire, Erin. A Fallen."

"Do you think Barty knows what's going on?"

"I think he's more likely than anyone to have a clue."

"You've been around as long as he has."

"But Barty is the nerd." Anya laughs. "He loves myths and legends, especially when it's to do with our kind."

"I hope he finds something. We're supposed to be planning a wedding."

"Hold the phone, you're what?"

Crap. We're such bad friends.

"Jesus, I'm sorry, Anya. We completely spaced. We decided to go ahead with the wedding before my thirtieth. Who knows what's around the corner? Things change. We never know what's going to happen next."

"Congratulations. And don't worry, I know you'd have called. It's not like you're having a Zen kind of time right now."

We laugh together. It's nice to feel some levity again.

"I think Amelia was a little surprised at first. But I just don't see the point in waiting."

"I couldn't agree more. Oh, I have a fantastic idea! Get married here."

"Here? What now?"

"Well, not this second." She giggles. "I know it's all a bit of a mess at the moment, but maybe that makes it the perfect time. As you said, you never know what's going to happen next."

The idea latches on to the part of me that wants to marry Amelia this very instant. I wanted something small, which is what it would be. Not quite Hawaii, but it's stunning, nonetheless. My parents come to mind, and the vision briefly steals my breath.

"Hey, what's that face for?"

"My parents," I stutter. "They—"

"Did you tell them? About us?"

I nod, not trusting my voice.

"Oh, Erin, I'm sorry."

"They were okay until this whole Fallen eating me thing came up."

"I think you should rephrase that," she mumbles with a raised eyebrow, causing me to laugh.

"Okay, not eating me. You know what I mean."

"Let me guess, they wanted to take you home with them?"

"Yes. It ended with them walking out."

Anya moves to sit next to me. "They're scared and reacting."

"That's what Amelia said."

"Because she's smart. If you want to get married here, we'll arrange for them to be flown over. If they decline, that's on them and something they will have to live with."

It would be something we'd all have to live with. I'm not sure my heart could take it if they rejected the invite.

"I'm not sure Amelia will want to do it now. You saw how she is."

"Maybe getting married to you is the one thing that *would* help."

I bite my lip in concentration and then yelp. I accidentally pierced the skin. Running my tongue over the small cut, I taste blood. Thankfully, it isn't making me turn nuts, so thank god for that.

As I trace my top lip, I pause. I cannot be feeling what I think I'm feeling. My mind screams for Amelia. How is this even possible? I feel like I'm saying that a lot recently. My hand flies to my mouth, covering it. Anya looks at me, alarmed. Standing, I want to run, but where the hell would I go?

Tires screeching to a halt over gravel echoes through the castle. The door bangs open and Amelia is next to me in seconds.

"What's wrong?" Her eyes are wild, just like before. "Is she here? Can you sense her?"

I shake my head. No, this feels so much worse. Lowering my hand, I tilt my head up. Amelia's eyes stay on mine briefly before tracking down to the cut on my lip. I draw back my top lip and wince when she gasps.

"How?" Amelia studies me with open concern. I know why she's struggling to comprehend what she's seeing. The same reason I am. Not only is the impossible happening, by that I mean I have...teeth unbefitting of my species. But these teeth are too long, even for a vampire.

I've studied vampire anatomy to help with my understanding of their world, their lives. A vampire's canines are a shade longer than humans, not like these. And they certainly don't drop or retract.

What *am* I?

Eight

It's times like this I wonder if I'm in an elaborate dream. One where vampires are still a myth, and I am none the wiser. If that were true, though, I wouldn't know what it was to find my soulmate, and that is unconscionable.

I was supposed to have another year until something like this happened. Then again, I'm not entirely sure something like this was ever supposed to happen.

I'm still baring my new teeth to Amelia, who looks dumbstruck. Neither of us knows what to do next. Thankfully, Anya steps up to the plate. She's calm and collected, unlike me. Inside, my stomach is in knots and my mind is frantic.

We still have too many unanswered questions, and clearly more arising every day. At this rate, I'm going to be a fully-fledged vampire in hours. A realization slams into my chest. I let a Fallen vampire feed from me. I understand that being changed into a vampire isn't possible that way, but what if? There are plenty of things happening to me that *shouldn't* be. And yet they are.

"Erin, sit down. Let me look." Anya removes my hand and tilts my head.

Running her finger over the tip of my canine—I refuse to see them as fangs—she presses firmly, causing her skin to be pricked. Studying her now bleeding index finger, Anya brings it to her mouth and sucks. I have no clue what the hell she's hoping to find out, but whatever it is, she's clearly puzzled.

"We need Barty."

"We need Dr. Mendhi," Amelia says, finally snapping out of her shock-induced trance.

"We need a priest," I comment quietly. It wasn't quiet enough. Amelia is on her knees in front of me moments later.

"You do not need a priest. You are not evil, Erin. We're not evil, you know that."

"We don't know what the fuck I am!" I didn't mean to bark at her, but I'm frustrated and scared.

"I know who and what you are, Erin. I've always known. You are mine, and I am yours. Whatever is happening, we will figure it out, but know I am here. Always by your side."

I bring our foreheads together, needing that closeness even just for a second. "Fetch the doctor. Anya, please call Barty."

They spring into action, which makes me smile temporarily until I feel my teeth again. Am I turning into a Fallen? Is that even possible?

Barty is the same level of calm as his wife when he arrives, which I appreciate.

"Erin, may I look?"

I nod, allowing him to examine me.

"Interesting."

"That's one word for it, I suppose."

"Did you feel anything?"

"Nope, nothing. One minute I had regular teeth and the next these."

"They're not overly elongated but definitely more than the average vampire. Sharp, too."

"They're producing some sort of chemical," Anya adds. "I tasted it when I pricked my finger."

"Really? May I?"

"You want me to bite your finger?"

"Yes, please."

Oh, for the love of god!

"Fine."

Of course, that's the moment Amelia returns with Dr. Mendhi, Mohan, and her parents. I can only imagine what it must look like.

"You're right, Anya. She is producing some sort of chemical."

"Really?" Dr. Mendhi is in front of me now, and I'm feeling antsy.

"Yes, definitely."

"I'm not biting anyone else!"

My tone is curt. I can see the disappointment on the doctor's face.

"Can't you extract it some other way?" I huff.

I'm not naïve enough to think I can get away from having tests done.

"I'll start with bloodwork. Then we will look at your new—"

"Fangs."

There, I said it.

"Teeth, my love. Not fangs." Amelia soothes.

"Let's not kid ourselves here. I know you believe you are nothing like the legends made up by humans, and you're right. But look at me, Amelia. I have fangs! Longer than yours. I let a vampire feed on me. I'm not one of you. I'm turning into a monster."

"You are not a monster." Amelia's voice is soft in my ear. Her arms circle around me and hold me tight. I hate that I'm breaking down in front of everyone, but there really is only so much a girl can take, you know.

"You are no monster," Barty says. "I believe you are the Salvator Regina, the Savior Queen."

"She's what now?" Lucille asks, barging into the room. "Sorry to interrupt, but I'm tired of being kept in the dark. What's happening?"

Instead of the peevishness Lucille usually radiates when kept out of the loop, all I see is concern.

"Lucille," Harlan admonishes.

"No, Father. We are here to help. None of us can do that when we don't know what the situation is."

"Where is Valentine?" Victoria asks, irked with her daughter's brashness.

"With Maria. She's fine."

Valentine is Harlan and Victoria's youngest child. She's almost three and as gorgeous as all her siblings. I was more than a little shocked to find out Victoria was pregnant at two hundred years old, but that's the life of an immortal.

"They might as well know," I interject.

"See, listen to Erin."

"Call the family in," Harlan commands.

Now I truly feel like a specimen waiting to be poked and prodded.

Amelia sits holding my hand as she fills in the rest of the clan. There's enough of us now to earn the name. Maybe I could come up with a coat of arms for us. Amelia's amused smile makes me blush. She's heard my musings, which aren't entirely appropriate for the situation we're in. I think my brain just needs an escape from all the seriousness.

"Are you okay, Erin?" Laurence, the oldest sibling, asks.

"Well, apart from being worried about constantly biting my lip, I'm fine."

That earns a titter.

"I'd like to know what's happening, though. Barty, you think I'm Regina, someone? Can you educate the class?"

"Of course." He mock bows. "It's a story of legend among the earlier vampires. They believed that a human woman with the ability to save all those who failed to find their mate would be born. Unlike humans, who struggle to comprehend that women are and always have been more suited to leadership, vampires rejoiced in her reign. She was celebrated and written into history. Unfortunately, most of it was lost. There are a handful of texts that name her, but that's all."

"She had the ability to save the Fallen?" I ask.

"Yes. Before we understood our biology, vampires relied on superstition. Gods and such, similar to humans."

I can't help but notice Dr. Mendhi perk up. There's that odd look of excitement again.

"And you think Erin is some kind of goddess?" Lucille couldn't keep the amusement out of her voice or off her face if she tried.

"Amelia thinks—"

"Not now," Amelia chastises. I was going to deliver a sarcastic and, once again, inappropriate response. One Lucille would have loved.

"No, I don't believe Erin is a deity." Barty smiles. "But I think there is some truth in it."

"I'll need to run tests." Dr. Mendhi is already scribbling in his notebook. He seems off, but I don't know why.

"Lovely, and while you're all trying to figure out what this is, I'm going to plan my wedding."

"Erin—"

"Nope, we're not waiting any longer. Anya has graciously offered the castle as a venue, and I'm happy to accept. I'll need help with organizing things."

"Erin."

"Amelia! This is happening. I refuse to go another week without being married to you. Please, give me this."

The room is silent and I should feel embarrassed for making a scene, but fuck it. I'm rapidly changing into a vampire who may or may not possess the ability to help Fallen vampires. I'm having a goddamn wedding.

"Okay. Let's get married."

"I'll need to steal you for a little while," Dr. Mendhi interrupts.

Party Pooper.

"Can it wait until tomorrow?" Amelia asks.

"I'd rather draw blood now. Also..." Dr. Mendhi reaches inside his jacket pocket and pulls out a small hip flask. Handing it to me, he nods his head. Flipping off the lid, I take two large gulps of Red. The more I taste it, the more I like it.

"Now what?" I ask, unsure of what he expects to happen.

Reaching forward, Dr. Mendhi gently lifts my upper lip. "Fascinating."

My tongue automatically traces my teeth. I suck in a breath. They're not pointy! Or long. My teeth are normal again.

"What the?"

"What the what?" Amelia is looking between the doctor and I.

"Look." I say, pointing to my mouth.

She leans forward and inspects my teeth. "What does this mean?"

"I'm not sure. It was just a hunch. I do, however, feel Erin will have to start a regimen of Red. Not the quantity you or I would drink, but a few mouthfuls a day. Until we know the reason all of this is occurring."

"How do you feel about that, my love?"

I shrug. "It's fine. It just tastes like water."

"Right." Barty claps. "I think it's time to open the whiskey now, don't you?"

A dozen heads nod. I definitely need a drink.

The room is spinning. Or is it me? Barty cracked open his special whiskey and we've all imbibed far too much.

Dr. Mendhi was a little put out that I only allowed him to take blood. If it were up to him, I'd be in his lab. Which I have no real problem with. I trust him and know it's important. Not just for me. If what Barty has shared has any truth to it, my recent changes could have an enormous impact on the vampire community.

But for one more night I just want to be Erin, human supreme, celebrating my upcoming nuptials to my sexy goddess of a fiancée.

"Sexy goddess, huh?"

Plastering a sultry grin on my face, I turn to Amelia. "Yes, sexy goddess."

"That should be your title, apparently."

"Oh, please."

"I do like it when you beg," she whispers in my ear.

A part of me is so relieved Amelia is getting frisky. It means she still loves me, wants me. Guilt still gnaws away at my heart every time I flash back to the garden and the woman. I didn't feel attracted to her in the romantic sense. But I *was* drawn to her, and that's enough to make me feel sick inside.

"I always want you, Erin. Please stop feeling bad. You did nothing wrong."

We kiss deeply. I need to feel her, to feel that connection that is solely ours.

"Please take me to bed."

I shriek as she flings me over her shoulder. I hear laughter and cheers. I also hear Lucille shout, "Good Lord, do they ever stop?"

My laughter drowns out the rest as Amelia sprints to our room. I've not even had the chance to take it all in yet. I thought a castle would be cold and drafty, but it's not at all. A fire is burning, casting a warm glow over the room. A large wooden four-poster bed stands proudly in the middle, sheets already turned down.

I'm lowered gently to the bed. Amelia's eyes are intense. "I will always love you."

"Thanks, Whitney." I giggle.

"I'm trying to be romantic, babe."

"Sorry, go on."

"No, you've ruined it now. I think I'll need to punish you for it."

"Yes, please."

"Erin! You're not supposed to be so excited about getting a spanking." She chuckles.

"Sorry," I pout. "Oh no, Amelia, please don't punish me."

She drops her head to my shoulder, laughing. "You're impossible."

"I'm adorable. Now, spank me. Or whip me. I don't care. Just touch me."

"Yes, my queen."

"That's going to become a thing, isn't it?"

"In the bedroom, yes. I like the idea of serving you."

"Hmm, in that case, maybe the spanking can wait. I think you'd better serve me on your knees."

"Fuck, Erin."

"That's the plan, honey."

Growling, Amelia stands and strips herself. I am more than happy to watch.

"I'm wet for you," she moans. Her hand is between her legs. I love it when she touches herself.

"On your knees, Amelia."

Dropping to the floor, she continues to touch herself lightly. Casting my clothes to the floor, I sit on the edge of the bed. Amelia's eyes are almost black. She's so turned on. My mouth waters at the sight of her ministrations.

It's only slight, but I feel my teeth elongate. That's a weird sensation, for sure.

"Oh shit, I need some Red."

I go to cover my mouth again, but Amelia stops me.

"Leave them out," she purrs.

Nine

Having the opportunity to watch Amelia sleep is a rare occurrence. We savored each other repeatedly last night, enough to keep her sleeping long after I wake.

It's possibly one of my creepier habits, but watching her like this, so relaxed, so vulnerable, is one of my favorite things to do. She's breathtaking, and she's mine.

Our lovemaking helped quell some fears I had. Listen to me using the word *quell*! That's what hanging around centuries-old vampires gets you. Anyway, I digress. Talking to Anya about Amelia helped some, but only Amelia's touch, her whispered words of love, could make a difference.

For my sanity, I need to talk to her about the vampire who fed on me. I know she's said there isn't anything to worry about, and I hope that's true. But we need to be completely transparent, and Amelia has been keeping me at bay in her mind, so there must be something more. She must be feeling more.

The rain is hammering the window. My mind wanders to the wedding. I think we might have to have an indoor service. Ireland is gorgeous, but the weather isn't a guarantee. Although, rain on your wedding day is supposed to be good luck, apparently. Ha, tell that to my cousin who found her husband banging their neighbor, Jeffrey. There was torrential rain on their wedding day.

"You look deep in thought, my love." Amelia's sleepy voice is yummy. All husky and... Jesus, what's got into me? We spent hours fucking each other last night, but my body still craves more. I crave her.

"Morning." I kiss her deeply, rolling on top of her. Amelia's hands snake around me, moving to my ass. She grabs both cheeks, pulling me further into her. I'm on fire! I make quick work of riling her up.

"You're in a good mood this morning," she moans.

My body is frenzied. I need her. Instead of replying, I guide my hand between her legs and take a long swipe through her wetness.

"Fuck!" she gasps.

My teeth elongate again, but this isn't like last night. Now I feel hungry for her. I can smell her blood, feel it coursing through her veins. My mind goes black. I'm losing control of myself, but I'm powerless to stop. Fingering her hard, I smile when she groans into my ear. I smile harder when I feel the blood pool in her pussy, engorging her further. Any restraint I have vanishes and I do the one thing I never thought I would. I bite Amelia.

Her scream is a mix of pain and pleasure, but I'm so lost in the feeling of taking her lifeblood into my mouth I pay little attention. It's only when I feel her go limp that something in the back of my mind pierces through the shadows.

My mind is back. I'm in control once more, and yet I kind of wish I wasn't. The sight of Amelia, unconscious and bleeding, renders me speechless.

I did that! I've hurt Amelia.

Grabbing my tank top from the floor, I press it hard to Amelia's neck with shaking hands. A few minutes pass and I almost cry when I feel Amelia move. Her eyes flicker open, and she looks dazed. Turning her head, she looks at me. Something unfamiliar flickers in her eye. I can't hear her thoughts. Is she blocking me? Oh my god, is she scared of me?

Backing away, I scramble off the bed. The cold air causes my naked body to shiver. Unable to look her in the eye, I find some sweatpants and a t-shirt. Dressed, I don't know what to do next. Amelia hasn't moved. She's just staring at me. The silence is killing me.

"I'm so sorry," I whisper before fleeing. It's clear to me now, I'm no longer safe to be around the people I love.

Nobody knows what's happening to me. Dr. Mendhi is at a loss. There isn't time to wait around hoping he finds something to explain all this, not when I've just attacked my soulmate. All this nonsense about being some sort of fucking savior queen is horseshit. I'm no savior. I'm turning into a monster. Maybe all the stories concocted through history about vampires aren't all false. Maybe humans got part of it right?

The castle is quiet as I race toward the front door. I have no idea where I'm going. All I know is that I need to leave. I have to get as far away from Amelia and our family as quickly as possible before I do something I can't come back from.

The rain is still pelting down as I leave the safety of the castle. Heading for Barty's garage, I head straight for his line of cars. Not the luxury ones. I'm not sure I can trust myself in one of those. An Audi will be fine. It's fast and automatic.

Once again, I have a voice in my head. This time it's telling me to stop being an idiot and go back to Amelia. But what if *that's* the voice that wants to harm her? I can't trust the words in my mind. I can't trust myself, full stop.

Gunning the engine, I don't look back as I speed off. How will Amelia explain this to her family? What the hell will they think of me for hurting her? And I know I hurt her. Fuck, I'll continue to hurt her just by staying away. Our souls need each other. The distance will hurt us both, but is my soul still intact? Am I being overly dramatic? Fuck!

Life was perfect before my birthday. I couldn't have wished for more, and now it's all gone to shit. The unfairness of it all keeps me company as I drive. I've no fucking idea where I'm going. I take turns now and then until eventually I have to stop. There is a pull in my heart, and I know it's Amelia searching for me.

∞

Once I block out the ache in my chest, I drive until I can't keep my eyes open. The events of the morning have drained me. The pub I find offers bed-and-breakfast, although I have no money. In my altered state, I left with only the clothes on my back and Barty's car. What a goddamn idiot.

Pulling into the pub's car park, I sit silently. What should I do? It's too dangerous to go back to the castle, right? I could attack someone. Jesus, I could hurt Valentine.

A dark thought germinates. How long will it take for me to descend completely into madness? As far as I'm concerned, that's the only logical reason for all of this.

Clearly, the Fallen has infected me? Turned me? I don't know, but everything went to shit the moment she turned up.

But what about the dreams?

Fuck, I was dreaming about biting Amelia before the Fallen drank from me. None of it makes any sense. Turning only happens on your birthday. You're *thirtieth* birthday.

My reverie is shattered when the car door opens. It's her again, but this time, she's sitting in the passenger seat.

"Please don't panic or scream."

Her voice is nothing like I remember. Gone is the desperation. She's beautiful, I'll give her that.

"Who are you?" My voice shakes.

"My name is Jordan. And I owe you my life."

So, the Fallen vampire has a name and a really nice haircut. Her eyes are golden now. She hardly resembles the frantic vampire I came across in the garden. But what does she want?

"How did you find me?"

I know the answer before I've finished asking the question. We're linked.

"You know how. You can sense me."

"Clearly not, because I didn't sense you getting into my car!"

"It's not your car." She grins. "I followed you from LA. We need your help."

"Who?"

"The Fallen. You're the key."

"Oh, for fuck's sake!" I've had it up to my eyeballs with all this shit. "I'm no key or savior. Okay? I can't help you."

"But you did. You literally saved me."

"Yeah and look where that's got me. What the hell did you do to me?"

Why am I even engaging this woman? Frustration boils up from deep within. Feeling claustrophobic, I tear off my safety belt and storm out of the car. The air is chilly, but at least the rain has stopped. There is a motorbike parked a few meters away. It's one of Barty's. This bitch has some nerve.

"I'm going to give it back. I wasn't expecting you to take off like that. What happened?"

"Listen, lady. I don't know you. I'm certainly not going to discuss personal things with you. Whatever you think I am, I'm not."

"You are. You cured me."

"It's not possible."

"And yet the proof is in front of you. I turned thirty, three months ago. I hadn't found my mate and was instantly taken into custody. It took mere hours for me to start falling. I remember all of it. The pain of my soul yearning for its other half was unbearable. The blackness taking over, voices whispering in my ear. The thirst. Shit, that was insufferable, and then I felt a spark. After months of pain, I felt a light grow in my chest. I felt you, Erin."

"How do you know my name?"

"I don't know. Just like I don't know how I found you in those gardens. All I remember is a surge of hope, strong enough to break my bonds. I didn't hurt anyone, just so you know. The hunger in me changed."

"I don't understand." Pacing back and forth, I must look crazy.

"Neither do I. But you can't deny the truth. After I found you, the connection was instant. You gave me your blessing to bite you, and the moment I drew blood, my rage ceased to exist. The voice evaporated into the ether. Your blood set me free from the worst kind of prison."

She is so earnest, I can't help but take in every word. Is she telling the truth? But what about my behavior? What effect is curing Jordan having on me?

"You left LA after you heard about the other escaped Fallen."

"Yes. My family thought it wise to leave for a while. Until we figured out what was happening."

"The other escaped Fallen is called Christopher. He's suffered for almost a decade. I found him. He was searching for you."

"Has he hurt anyone?"

"No. But he needs you, Erin."

The pull in my heart increases to the point where I grab my chest. Amelia is in pain. But so is Christopher. I don't know this guy, but my gut tells me I should go with Jordan. My head and heart are conflicted. I want nothing more than to drive back to the arms of my soulmate. To soothe her.

"Amelia would understand."

"Don't speak of her." My tone is final. I get there is a link between Jordan and me, but it is flimsy at best, nothing compared to what I share with Amelia.

"I'm sorry. I wasn't trying to—"

"Yes, you were. Understand one thing, Jordan. Amelia is my mate. We share a bond deeper than anything you could imagine. Never assume you know what either of us would think or want."

"I apologize, Erin. Truly. But please, come with me and help Christopher. He needs you more than Amelia right now."

I hate to agree with her, but I do. If she is telling the truth, this Christopher guy has been in hell for the past ten years.

"Where is he?"

"Dublin. We stowed away." They must have been desperate to risk leaving the States. Every vampire in LA is looking for them.

Closing my eyes, I open my mind to Amelia. *Trust me, my love. This is for the best.*

I can only hope she hears me and understands.

Ten

I'm clearly making unhinged decisions. I wish I could blame it on my menses, like I do most of the time I act nuts, but this is way beyond that. Swanning off with a Fallen vampire is stupid. I know it, but I'm still doing it. For right or wrong, I know I have to do this.

We left Barty's car and motorcycle at the pub. No doubt they will be easily traced. I'm surprised I didn't get caught, to be honest. I half expected Barty and Amelia to show up the moment I parked.

Jordan opted to drive. The car she "acquired" is a late-model Beetle. What's a little grand theft auto in the grand scheme of things? My skull is pounding with the effort it's taking to block Amelia. I hate doing it, but it's for her safety. It is, isn't it? And I'm making the right decision to leave her, aren't I? My heart is screaming at me in revolt.

The journey so far has been relatively silent. Jordan has tried several times to strike up a conversation, but I'm too tired and anxious to participate. The quicker we get to Christopher, the quicker I can help him. That's the only thing I can think about, the only thing bringing me some peace of mind. Once that's done, I can try to figure out what to do next. Maybe I could call the doctor discreetly?

I must have drifted off, because when I come around, we're entering Dublin. The car pulls into an industrial estate on the outskirts of the city. Could this be any sketchier? I doubt it.

"Hey, it's not like we could hire an Airbnb."

Great, can Jordan read my thoughts too?

"Unscrew your face, will ya?" she snarks.

Okay, maybe not. Our link is still tentative, just the way I want it to stay. I can handle her sensing me, but not invading my thoughts again. Only my mate has the right to do that.

"Couldn't you find somewhere a little less...murder-y?"

Jordan lets out a shock of laughter. "Because he's so vulnerable? Erin, the last thing any of us want is

Christopher within reach of humans. I made sure he was secure before leaving him. This place has been abandoned for a while. There aren't even any squatters."

"Fine, you're right."

Why did I even bring it up? Of course, Jordan and Christopher would need to stay out of the way, and an abandoned building was the right call.

"Take me to him."

Jordan wastes no time. She slips out of the car, not even bothering to shut the door behind her. Following, I try to tap into that feeling. The one I had when Jordan was near. We enter the dilapidated factory, and I instantly feel him. Oh god, he is in so much pain, I almost double over. I can feel it in my stomach. Scorching heat ripples through my body. Fuck, is this what he feels all the time?

Sensing my thought path, Jordan takes me gently by the arm and hurries us through the cavernous rooms. Christopher must be deep inside. Smart. At least that way, if by any chance some poor soul came across the building, it would be unlikely they'd accidentally find Christopher.

We turn the corner into what must have been some kind of workshop. Brick columns hold up the roof and attached to one of them is the saddest and most horrific sight I have ever seen. Christopher.

"He's in a really bad way," Jordan comments unnecessarily.

It takes me one quick glance to see he is in a poor state. It's not just his blood-red eyes and pleading expression. It's everything. Considering he is supposed to be over thirty, I could easily mistake him for a gangly teen. There isn't an ounce of meat on his bones.

His hair touches his collarbones that are protruding unnaturally. Scars mar every inch of his body.

"Why isn't he dressed?"

The man is only wearing underwear.

"He can't stand it on his skin. I had the fight of my life just getting boxers on him."

We approach slowly. I see him muttering to himself, his eyes searching the room feverishly. I need him to focus. When Jordan focused on me, I could hear her. She took over my mind. Christopher is so frantic, I can't get a read on him or make a connection.

"Chris," Jordan whispers. Her hand slowly touches his head. As if electrocuted, Christopher recoils with a wail.

My god.

"Christopher?" I keep my voice soft. His eyes snap to mine and I know I have him.

"Help me," he pleads.

"Help me untie him."

Christopher might be almost naked, but most of his body is wrapped in tight chains, anchoring him to the column.

"Are you sure?" Jordan looks worried, but I'm not. Now Christopher is centered on me, I know he won't try to run. Hell, why would he? The man escaped to find me. I just hope I can help him like I did Jordan.

"Yes, take off the chains."

Jordan works fast as I support Christopher's withered body. He weighs nothing. Finally, the last chain hits the floor with an ear-piercing clang that echoes for several seconds.

Lowering him to his knees, I settle in front of him. "Hold his head up."

Jordan does as I say without question. Once again, my instincts kick in. This time, I know Christopher doesn't need to bite me. It's the other way around.

My teeth elongate, and I feel the chemical compound form at the tips. Christopher is shaking so badly Jordan has to use her considerable strength to keep him still.

"It's okay, Christopher. It's okay."

"Please," he whispers, and I wonder if he is about to pass out.

Leaning forward, I bring my mouth close to his neck. A pulsing ache rises in my throat. My mind goes black, just as it did with Jordan. I see red swirls, like blood in water. It overtakes my senses.

I feel him relax the second my teeth pierce his skin. His shaking stops and he leans into me. The first draw of his blood makes me cringe. Not because I'm drinking blood, but because it tastes tainted. Poisoned. Taking several more draws, I concentrate with everything I have. The last thing I want to do is drain him, but I know I have to take out enough to let my...what, venom? Serum? Whatever it is I'm producing, it has to be in sufficient quantity to dilute Christopher's contaminated blood.

Like a bell ringing in my ear, I know I need to stop. I've taken enough. Retracting my teeth, I pull away. Jordan gently lays Christopher down. He looks to be sleeping. Sitting back on my haunches, I absentmindedly wipe my mouth. There's only a drop of his blood on my lips. Clearly, I'm a clean biter!

"What now?" Jordan is sitting cross-legged next to him, looking at me.

"We wait," I say.

At least I think that's what we should do. This is so different from my encounter with Jordan. Now, I feel a sense of responsibility.

"How are you?"

She looks at me like I'm the second coming. "You did it again."

I'm momentarily distracted by her eyes. The golden hue is fading. She has naturally green eyes. Does this mean the color is a direct result of the link to me? That it's temporary, but the bond remains. Huh, well, I guess it's better than walking around with golden orbs attracting unwanted attention.

"Did what?"

"Saved a damned soul."

"Damned? Is hell real?"

"If you felt even a second of what Christopher was feeling, you know the answer to that."

"He was like that for ten years?"

Jordan nods. "I can't even imagine. I had a few months, and I was ready to end it all."

"Why didn't you?"

She laughs mirthlessly. "You really believe the good doctor would allow his test subjects to die?"

Her words pull me up short. What does she mean? Is she referring to Dr. Mendhi?

"Please explain." I try to keep my voice even.

"We're led to believe the Fallen are mindless creatures, only capable of hurting. I believed that growing up until it happened to me."

Reaching forward, I lay my hand on her arm. "Go on."

"Yes, the thirst for human blood is unbearable, but the worst part is you know what's happening. Your mind is fogged with rage and pain, but you are still the vampire you were before falling. That is the worst kind of torture."

"Dear god."

"I wanted to die every day, and he knew it. Fuck, he knows so much more than he tells the council."

"I don't understand."

What is she talking about?

"Dr. Mendhi. He's a special kind of sick fuck."

"But...he's—"

"Helpful? Only to the council and higher families. In my lucid moments at the beginning of my change, I'd listen to him rant on about lower classes. He's insane and obsessed with the Fallen. Christopher was tortured for ten years. You've seen the scars."

"But?" I can't process what she's telling me.

I knew he was doing illegal experiments. We found that out when Amelia was suffering side effects. Dr. Mendhi gave us a serum, and now I know who he experimented on. My gut tightens and I feel the vomit rushing up from my stomach.

Scrambling away, I unload behind the brick pillar. How fucking shortsighted were we? Me and the entire Loch family looked away as Dr. Mendi did god knows what to the Fallen. And we didn't bat an eyelid. All we cared about was Amelia.

"He doesn't want to cure us," Jordan continues quietly. "He wants us as permanent lab rats. Do you really think he spent all his time trying to come up with a cure?"

"Yes!"

She laughs maniacally. "That man uses the Fallen for everything. All his crazy concoctions are tried and tested on them. On me!"

"I didn't know."

"I know, but now you do!" Jordan looks down at Christopher, who looks so peaceful. "You have to do something, Erin. There are cages full of vampires like him. Some have been there for decades."

Cages?

"What can I do?"

"They have felt you," she says, looking at me with a kind of hope that scares me. "I don't know how you do what you do, Erin, but you are our savior. I felt it, Christopher felt it, and so did the other Fallen. They need you!"

Well, shit! I don't want to believe her. In fact, I want to forget about all this, go to the castle, grab Amelia and go home.

Jesus, Amelia. I need to figure out what the hell I'm doing. I can't stay away from her forever. Neither of us can survive it. Literally. But how do I stop myself from hurting her?

And how the hell do we figure this out without the doctor? I need to tell Mohan. He needs to be stopped. I need...I need—

"Whoa, Erin, calm down." Jordan is grabbing my shoulders.

I've started to pace. When did that happen? My breathing is labored, and my mind feels like a hive of wasps has settled in.

"Deep breaths."

Focusing on Jordan's eyes, I take several calming lungs full of air. But it isn't enough. I need Amelia. Closing my eyes, I slowly lift the barrier in my mind. Amelia's pain rushes through me in an unstoppable wave.

"Oh god," I breathe. What have I done?

"Hey, hey, calm down. Sit here." Jordan lowers me to the floor, close to Christopher.

"I have to go back. Amelia, she's suffering."

I thought I'd have more time than this. Amelia is strong. I thought she'd...what? Cope better with my absence?

Fuck, I'm a moron. Of course she isn't. Lucille warned me once that if I ever left Amelia, it would kill her. And it is! I can feel the consequence of my disappearance keenly.

"What are you going to tell them?" Fear laces every syllable. Jordan's face is ashen.

"Nothing about you or Christopher. I have to get to Amelia."

"Erin, listen to me. If the doctor finds out about you, and what you can do, he will find a way to exploit you for his purposes. No matter who you are, he's obsessed."

"But—"

"I know Amelia is suffering. I can feel her, too."

"What?"

Eleven

"What the hell do you mean, you can feel her?"

My panic is replaced by rage. No one has the right—

"You and Amelia are one," Jordan rushes to explain. "I can feel her, just as I can you. It's not the same as your bond, Erin, it's weaker. But we are linked, possibly permanently. I can't help it."

Blowing out a frustrated breath, I sit back down. God knows how long Christopher will be out. Is this the first time in ten years the man has found a slice of peace?

"Sorry. I just feel on edge."

That's an understatement, if ever I heard one.

"Understandable." Jordan is still tense. She is keeping her guard up.

"I honestly don't know what to do for the best."

I've made such a mess of everything.

Scooting closer, Jordan squeezes my shoulder. "You need to be smart, Erin."

"Meaning?"

"Be wary of who you trust. Dr. Mendhi has friends in high places, you know that!"

"I trust Amelia and our family."

"And the Grand Master?"

There is no way Mohan would sanction such atrocities against his own kind. "I trust him."

"But there are those amongst us that want change."

"Spit it out, Jordan." My patience is waning.

"You've heard of the dissension growing within the families."

"Those who wish to expose vampires to the world."

"Yes, and I have to agree with them. We don't deserve to live in the shadows, denying who we are."

"Okay?" I'm not sure where she is going with this.

"Those people would want to meet you, Erin. Think about it. The one reason the council has point-blank refused to entertain vampires outing themselves is because of the Fallen. The minute humans find out about the Fallen, there would be those who wish them harm. That would be all it took to cause chaos for our kind."

"Agreed."

"But you are the key!"

"I really wish you'd stop calling me that."

"How can you not see it? You have the power to save us."

"We have no idea what I have. Christopher hasn't even woken up yet. He could still be nuts."

"No, and you know that. In your gut you know he's okay now."

Damn it, she's right again. "Fine, carry on."

"If the Fallen no longer pose a threat, the vampires calling for change have what they need to persuade the council."

"You really think vampires should expose themselves?"

"I suppose. We've helped shape the world as much as humans. They might think they're the alphas, but we know differently."

"That sounds like you believe vampires are better than humans, Jordan. Are you forgetting I'm still human?"

"I think nothing of the sort. I just want my kind to live freely in the world. You should know by now vampires are communal. We love and help each other. Don't you think humanity could do with our guidance?"

Well, she's not wrong. But it's foolish to think it would be that simple.

"I guess. But that's a long way off."

"True. Yet we are a step closer to that with you."

"Only if the council sees it as a positive thing."

My gut is talking to me again. I can't see how Dr. Mendhi got away with his behavior for so long without anyone knowing.

"You think the council is privy to Mendhi's experiments?"

I look at her, weighing up my response. "It's possible. I still believe Mohan is trustworthy, though."

Jordan sighs. "All of this is guesswork. You're right. We need to get you back to Amelia. But, and this is important to acknowledge. Half the vampire population is looking for Christopher and me. If they find you with us, I don't know what they'll do."

"I can explain."

"And what if they're with the doctor? You would put yourself in danger."

"So what the fuck do you suggest?"

I feel like a spring ready to snap.

"We make our way to the castle. Get to Amelia without anyone being the wiser."

"We?"

"I think it's a good idea to stick together."

"Jordan, there is no we. I'm... I don't know what you're expecting from me, but I can't be responsible for you."

"I never asked you to be, Erin. As you mentioned earlier, you're still human. The people looking for us, and you, are not. Let us protect you until we get you to Amelia."

I sense there is more to Jordan's need to stay with me than simple protection. If I tap into our connection, I feel her loneliness.

Before I have the chance to answer, Christopher stirs. Jordan helps to sit him up. Relief washes through me when I see his beautiful amber eyes staring back at me. I wonder how long they'll stay that color. It really is beautiful. Even in his disheveled and emaciated state, I can already see a glow on his skin.

"Erin," he breathes.

"Shh, it's okay. Just stay still. You need to rest."

The guy needs way more than rest. He needs food.

"Jordan, he needs Red."

"I have some. Hold on." Leaving us, Jordan rushes to the car.

"How are you feeling?"

Christopher answers with a sob. I reach for him and take him into my arms. The breakdown was an inevitability. No one, human or vampire, could endure what he has and not fall apart.

Sitting silently, I rock him until eventually his tears stop. Sitting up, he takes my face in his hands and looks deep inside me. I can feel him touching my soul.

"I can never repay what you have done for me, Erin. Know I'm in your debt for eternity."

"Christo—"

"I'll stay by your side until you order me to go."

"We're taking her back to the castle," Jordan interjects, sitting down, handing him a black bottle I know contains Red. He nods his thanks and drinks greedily.

"My god, that's good."

"So no hankering after human blood?" I ask in a teasing voice because the weight of his words still sits on me, making me uncomfortable.

Screwing up his face, Christopher mock gags. "Jesus, no."

"Keep drinking," Jordan urges. "We need you to gain some strength before we leave."

"Did you tell her about the doctor?" Christopher's face portrays his hatred for the man.

"I did." Jordan places her hand on his in comfort.

"Chistoph—"

"Call me Chris."

"Chris, I didn't know. Well, not the extent."

Guilt drills through my stomach lining, threatening a repeat session of vomiting.

"Erin," he begins, and I hate that he is trying to comfort me. "There are plenty of people aware of his experiments who turn a blind eye."

"They know the true nature of what he does?"

The idea anyone would know and say nothing is disgusting.

"Not his true reason for taking the Fallen. But vampires aren't stupid. They know he needs them to experiment on, to produce a cure."

"But he's not doing it for a cure, is he?"

Chris shakes his head. "No."

Even if that were the case, we, I, was wrong for turning away from his behavior. The Fallen deserved more from us.

"Before we worry about all that, we need to find transport and figure out how to get back to the castle without every vampire from here to the U.S. finding out."

Jordan is right. Damn, does she ever get tired of it?

"I'll find us some wheels. The Beetle isn't safe anymore."

With that, Jordan leaves.

"Jesus," I whisper.

"She's a force." Chris laughs.

We fall silent for a while. Both of us have our own shit going on, and sometimes words aren't necessary. I peek under the veil in my mind again, needing to feel Amelia's connection. Steeling myself, I wait for the pain. It hits me like a ton of bricks, but I stay strong. Amelia needs to know I'm okay and I'm coming home.

A soft glow emanates from the dark depths of my subconscious and I know she's heard me. I hope I've given her a little reprieve. How is she ever going to forgive me? I need to break from my rapidly souring thoughts.

"How did you escape?"

In the state I saw him, it's a wonder he could even walk, let alone escape from whatever hell hole he was kept in.

"I honestly couldn't tell you. All I know is I felt a light pass through me. It cut through the pain and voices. Kind of like a guide. My mind became clear, and I knew I had to find you. The next thing I know, I'm in an alleyway, and Jordan is helping me to my feet."

"You blacked out?"

Understandable.

"Yes, I think so."

My mind ponders on Jordan's revelation. If she and Chris felt this "light," does that mean the other Fallen are feeling it, too? If so, will there be a mass breakout?

"Yes, they felt it." Chris smiles at me shyly.

"You can hear me?"

"Not really. I can almost sense your words, but that's it."

"A group of Fallen vampires on the loose is going to be bad, Chris. The council will send everyone, and I doubt they'll stop to ask questions once they find them."

"No, it'll be a massacre. That's why you must find someone to tell. Someone who will help."

"Mohan. I trust him."

"Me, too."

Huh, that's a surprise.

"Why?"

124

"The good doctor liked to rant about the Grand Master being shortsighted."

"You remember?"

"Yes. There were times of lucidity, which only added to the mental pain."

"Surely the vampires who wish to be out in the open should be our first port of call."

But then again, Mohan is the one with the power. He could stop all of this.

"Let's see if we can get to Amelia first. Then we'll worry about everything else," Jordan reiterates as she returns. I wonder if she's former military. Her attitude and body language would say so.

"Should we wait for dark?" That's the extent of my input. I have no idea how to be stealthy or whatever. I just want to be in Amelia's arms.

"We need to eat and rest. Then we'll go. Erin, I got you a burger and fries. Chris, you and I get some fresh Red *and* a burger."

I'm a little disappointed I'm not having Red, which in itself is disconcerting.

Chris clinks his bottle to Jordans. "Nice!"

"What car did you get?" How many crimes have we committed so far? I should probably be more worried than I am about that.

"Ford Focus. It's not flashy or new."

Yeah, this isn't Jordan's first rodeo.

My appetite is nonexistent, but I force the burger down. Jordan and Chris devour their food and sip happily on their Red. Both sense my rising impatience and thankfully it's enough to convince Jordan it's time to head out.

The day is almost over as I help lower Chris into the back seat of the car. He's looking much better, but a couple of bottles of blood and fast food aren't going to undo the neglect he's faced. Time and care will do that.

As on the journey to Dublin, the car is silent as we drive. I just can't seem to get a handle on anything. So much has happened in such a short amount of time. My mind wanders to Amelia. I've lifted the block several times to do a quick check-in. I sense her relief that I'm okay, but I also feel something else. God, I wish I knew what it was, but unless I open my mind entirely, I'm going to have to wait.

Jordan makes several quick turns. Her face has taken on a serious frown.

"What's wrong?"

"We're being followed."

"Maybe they're people we can trust?" I already know the answer to that by Jordan's scowl. Chris is fast asleep still.

"No. We need to lose them."

"How do you—"

"Trust me," Jordan almost growls and sticks her foot on the gas pedal. The car shoots forward. Chris wakes up looking confused. It takes him a second, but eventually he understands what's going on.

"How far are we from the castle?"

If we can just make it there, I know Barty and Mohan will help.

"Too far. We can't outrun them on the highway."

Without a second thought, Jordan pulls some *Fast and Furious* shit that leaves me hanging onto the door. If we survive this particular car chase, we're going to have a conversation.

Twelve

C ar sickness has never been a problem until this very second. Jordan is throwing us around every bend. Where are all the police in Dublin? There's no way we haven't been picked up on a speed camera or twelve.

Whatever maneuvers she's doing seems to work. The black SUV that was trailing us can't keep up with Jordan's sharp turns. Neither can my stomach.

"Not long," Jordan shouts over another ear-shattering tire squeal.

"To the left, they'll never make that," Chris shouts.

The pair seem to be enjoying themselves. Jordan slams on the brakes, pitching us to the left. My face hits the window and definitely leaves an Erin-shaped face smudge.

Sure enough, the SUV tries to stop in time, but sails past the turn, giving Jordan enough time to make a clean getaway.

"That was close." Jordan checks her rearview mirror constantly.

"That was horrible!"

"That was fucking awesome," Chris hollers, pumping his bony fist.

"Clearly we have different ideas of awesome."

"I'm going to find an alternative route to the castle. One through the back roads."

Jordan is still in evasion mode. Christ, when did my life become this?

We drive for miles, Jordan constantly turning. I have zero idea where we are in relation to Barty and Anya's. Eventually, my anxiety gets the best of me.

"Do you know where we are?"

Jordan side-eyes me and that's when I know she, like me, has no clue where we are.

"Pull over in the next village. We need a map."

The village is small. I see one shop that might provide us with what we need. Both Jordan and I agree that Chris should remain in the car. He's still too weak, and it doesn't take three grown adults to find a map.

Stepping into the street, I feel a pressure on the small of my back as we walk. Jordan's hand is warm to the touch. My mind tells me that her familiarity is a byproduct of our bond, but the way she's looking at me right now...maybe there's more to it. My heart belongs to Amelia, but I can't deny that the closeness of Jordan is a balm.

Shaking my head, I refocus my mind. This isn't the time to be analyzing. We have to get to the castle.

Now, even I know it would be stupid to try to use a phone. People can trace them, right? A paper map seems like a better choice. I've never used a physical map before, but surely it can't be that difficult.

Thankfully, I didn't voice my opinion out loud, because it turns out, map reading is really fuckin' difficult. It took me a solid ten minutes just to locate the village we'd stopped in.

"Do you want me to look?" Jordan's been itching to take over, but I need something to occupy my mind, so I stubbornly hold on to the map.

"Ha, look, we're here and there is Barty's place."

"We drove further than I thought," Jordan mumbles, studying the different roads.

"Won't they expect us to go there?" Chris asks, his head leaning back on the car seat, eyes closed. His energy levels come in peaks and troughs.

I'm growing frustrated again. "We don't know who *they* are. That's the problem."

Aren't we just running round in circles with all this constant guessing?

"It was the doctor's guys. Trust me, Erin. I could smell them."

"Smell them?"

Jordan nods. "Since the change. You know, from crazy to sane, my senses are heightened. I'll never forget the scent of those fuckers."

"Me too," Chris adds darkly.

"So if they're with the doctor, it's a safe bet they weren't going to take us back to the castle."

"I doubt it. I wonder what they would've done with you though," Chris remarks. I turn in my seat to look at him. "I'm not sure even the doctor would mess with you."

"Amelia would rip his spine out," Jordan scoffs.

"Not just that, but the doctor would be messing with one of the most powerful families, who are also extremely close to the council and Grand Master. If he wants to continue his fucked up work, he needs to keep off their radar. Or at least make them believe his work is all to do with finding a cure."

Chris wipes a hand down his face in exhaustion. Even a brief chat is enough to drain him.

"Then we must get to Amelia. Tell her everything and get Mohan on board."

"Careful. We still don't know if any of the council are a part of Mendhi's weird science club," Jordan cautions.

"Jesus, this feels so unreal. It just doesn't happen in normal life, right? All this conspiracy crap!"

"Says the woman who knows vampires exist." Chris chuckles.

Okay, fair point.

I breathe out a long sigh, hoping to expel the residual adrenaline still beating around my body. The last few hours had been a rush, but not a good one.

"We're about two hours away from the castle. I say we find somewhere to eat, gather our strength, and then go. By the time we arrive, it will be late. Hopefully, most of the family, and more importantly, the doctor, will be in bed."

"Okay, it's a plan." Jordan switches off the car, already opening the door. "There's a pub a few streets back. We can grab some food."

"I'd like some Red, too." It's out of my mouth before I have time to stop it.

Truthfully, though, that dull ache at the back of my throat has been growing. The last thing I want to do is hurt someone, like I did with Amelia. The knot of guilt coils tighter. I'm scared that if I don't keep the ache under control, I'll do something stupid. What happens if I attack Chris or Jordan?

"No problem." Jordan levels me with a look. I'm not sure what she's trying to convey, but my mind buzzes with support, so I guess that's it. She's not judging me or asking questions. Chris is smiling at me widely, which is odd.

"Welcome to the club, Erin." He grins. I roll my eyes playfully.

We end up going to the pub for an hour after we've had our fill of Red. I feel like a teenager again, drinking secretly in the car, as if my parents might catch me.

The first sip took me by surprise. In a good way. I had to restrain myself from gulping it down. I felt a little self-conscious at first, wondering what Jordan and Chris were thinking, but they chatted and laughed without giving me and my bottle of Red a second thought. I'm grateful to them both. This is a new side of my...condition? I need to be okay with it. If drinking Red is the only way to stop me from hurting people, then I'll drink it happily.

A bell sounds from behind the bar. "Last orders, folks. Drink up."

"Looks like it's time," Jordan mutters. Chris and I nod our heads. This is all feeling very cloak and dagger, which is making me want to laugh nervously.

"How can you not like pineapple on pizza?" Chris bellows from the backseat.

The pizza-topping conversation has been ongoing for miles, with Jordan and Chris getting more and more heated. Chris is the pineapple guy, and Jordan is the anchovy girl. I hate anchovies but have wisely chosen to stay out of their bickering.

"Erin, tell her she's nuts."

Or maybe not.

"I like pineapple on pizza."

"And anchovies?" Jordan shoots.

"Sorry, it's a no from me. But Marcus, Laurence, and Aliah love them."

"Ha, I win," Chris singsongs.

"You both suck," Jordan pouts.

As juvenile as the conversation is, it's been nice to talk and laugh about something mundane. Although, I have come to realize that Chris and Jordan bicker like kids, and I'm the adult. Even though both of them are older than me. I still have this sense of responsibility for them both, which I can only chalk up to the link we share. I wonder if I'm their...mother in some way? Does that sound crazy? It's like I created them. Well, that's how it feels inside. Okay, I'll add that nutty thought to all the others bouncing around my brain.

Suddenly, a pull on my conscience steals my breath. Amelia is in pain. A lot of pain. Oh god.

"Jordan, you need to drive faster."

She doesn't question me, and I think she and Chris felt the jolt, too.

As the signposts fly by, I do my best to track us on the map. Safe to say, I'm not orientationally gifted. My heart lightens briefly when we drive through the town, two away from the castle. Lifting my veil, I connect with Amelia's struggling mind.

I'm so close, baby. Hang on.

Jordan pulls to a stop before entering the castle grounds. We'd already decided it would be wise to ditch the car and go on foot. Looking at my watch, I see it's late enough that everyone should be in their rooms. Hopefully.

Chris is still weak but can walk by himself unaided. We creep over the grass, and I'm suddenly hit with the urge to laugh again. I need to get my shit under control.

There are several rooms still lit up, but most of them are on the upper floors. Mine and Amelia's room is one of them that is illuminated.

"Barty doesn't have dogs or anything, does he?" Chris whispers.

"No," Jordan answers for me. I forget she's cased the joint before. I can't wait to tell Amelia. I've just used the phrase case-the-joint in a serious setting.

"We'll go to the kitchen." There is a small side door that leads to the kitchen. Amelia and I have used it several times when we wanted to escape the family for a little while. Before we enter, I have a thought. "If you guys have enhanced senses, surely everyone in there will too," I say, pointing to the door. "We're seriously trying to sneak past a gaggle of vampires?"

"A gaggle? Is that what we're called?" Chris asks seriously.

"No, it's a coven," Jordan whispers back.

"Focus," I hiss. "How can we possibly get past them without them hearing or smelling us?"

"Relax," Jordan soothes. "Chris and I are an exception. Whatever you've done to us has enabled those changes. The family, council, and the doctor all have slightly heightened senses. Nothing too far from humans, so we'll be fine."

Let's add that minor revelation to the collection of unanswered "what the fucks" I'm storing in my mind vault.

Nodding, I try the door handle. It's open, as I hoped it would be. Barty told us he's been meaning to get the lock fixed for close to ten years but always forgets. I'm grateful he didn't find the time over the past few days to finally get the job done.

The kitchen is dark and cold. A shiver runs through me. We stop every few seconds to listen. At the top of the kitchen stairs, we come across our first obstacle. Barty must still be in his office. There is soft jazz playing, which I know he enjoys with a few glasses of whiskey.

"Wait there," I whisper. If I get caught, it's no big deal. I hope. But if either Jordan or Chris get caught, I don't know what the hell will happen.

Tiptoeing into the hall, I peek to see if the office door is open. It's ajar, but not enough to reveal us. Waving the others over, we proceed. Thankfully, the rest of the castle's lower floor is in darkness.

Now, we just need to get to Amelia's room. Only the staircase to go. However, if we get caught on that, we won't have many places to run.

I catch a look shared between Jordan and Chris. Chris nods and then turns to me.

"I'm going to pick you up," Jordan says matter-of-factly. "Where is Amelia's room?"

"What? Why are—"

"Trust us," Chris begs.

"It's the fourth on the left."

My sentence is barely out of my mouth when Jordan scoops me up. Literally. I stifle a gasp and then hold on for dear life. Jordan wasn't lying when she said she has enhanced abilities. We're at the top of the stairs and outside Amelia's door before I have the chance to utter a word.

Holy shit, Jordan and Chris are *fast*. I'm talking super-fast.

Setting me down gently, I can't help but stare at them in shock. We are definitely going to have a talk! But that needs to wait. My attention is drawn to the pulsing cries of Amelia's soul behind that door, and I almost fall to the floor.

A steadying hand squeezes my shoulder. "You're okay. Go to her." Chris's voice is soft and calming.

Pushing the door open slowly, I slip into the room. Amelia is lying prone on our bed. The covers up to her chest, and if I couldn't feel her soul, I'd think she was dead.

Thirteen

The light in Amelia's room is low, but enough that I see how pale she is. Her face looks skeletal. What the fuck happened to her?

Crossing the room, I pass Lucille unnoticed until I'm suddenly thrust up the wall, her hand around my throat. Is she fucking growling at me?

"I warned you."

"Luc—"

"I told you what would happen if you left her. Look at her Erin. Look at your mate." Lucille's voice is barely above a whisper but the malice laced in every word shocks me.

Tears well in my eyes as they drift from Lucille's raging gaze to Amelia.

Oh god, what have I done?

"Let me down," I beg. I need to get to her, hold her in my arms, and make things better.

"I should rip your fucking throat out," Lucille spits, and my irritation rises. I may have fucked up by leaving in the first place, but Lucille is now keeping me from my mate.

An unnaturally powerful wave of anger fills me from head to toe. Grabbing Lucille's hand that is still clamping my esophagus shut, I break her grip with ease.

Looking at me in surprise, I take advantage of Lucille's break in concentration and push her back. I didn't think I'd put that much effort into it, but by the way Lucille sails across the room, I'd say there are a few more things about my condition that I need to look into.

Her body hits the floor with a thud. Ignoring her deer-in-headlights expression, I rush to Amelia. The room blurs as I run to her, climbing on the bed. Amelia lies still, seemingly unaware of her surroundings.

Dropping my lips to her ear, I desperately try to coax her awake. Nothing. She's not responding to my voice, so I do the next best thing. Closing my eyes, I put my forehead to hers, and lift my mind veil entirely, searching for her.

My mind is silent. Calling her name, I wait and wait. She's not there. Oh god. Shuffling behind me makes me turn. Victoria and Harlan stand looking at me. I can't tell if they want to take me into their arms or rip me limb from limb. I couldn't blame them if it was the latter. Look what I've done to their daughter.

"Erin," Victoria whispers softly.

"What happened?" I choke.

Harlan crosses the room and helps Lucille to her feet.

"We'd like to know the same thing. Where have you been, and why on earth did you leave?"

I look at them, baffled. Amelia didn't tell them I attacked her. Swallowing hard, I kiss Amelia gently on the lips and slip off the bed. Drawing myself to my fullest height, which against the Loch giants isn't very impressive, I walk to Victoria.

"I bit her."

Her eyebrows furrow and I know she's conversing with Harlan trying to figure out what that means.

"Erin, I don't understand."

"I'm changing, Victoria. I attacked Amelia. I daren't stay. I was so terrified I'd do it again and seriously hurt her. I panicked and ran."

"What do you mean by attacked her?" Lucille asks, her tone cold.

Turning to her, I stare just as coldly back. "I mean, we were making love. I felt something change in me and I bit her. I almost drank her dry. Fortunately, I stopped in time...in time to see Amelia look at me with fear." My voice breaks as I remember Amelia's look.

"Amelia could never be afraid of you, Erin," Harlan gently replies.

"She was." I know what I saw and nobody will convince me otherwise. "Now, can you tell me what happened to her?"

"What do you think?" Lucille shoots.

"I don't know," I grind out. "Maybe if you fucking tell me."

"Okay, okay," Victoria interrupts. "Harlan, can you get Moha—"

"No! Victoria no. You can't. Please, just trust me. There are things we need to talk about. As a family."

Lucille scoffs and I'm ready to launch her out the fucking window.

"Alright. Can we wake the rest of the family?"

"Not just yet. Please, tell me what happened."

"It was like the first time," Harlan begins. "But in fast-forward. Within hours of your departure, Amelia was coughing up blood. The only thing we could do was sedate her in the end."

"Has she been awake since?"

"In and out. We've tried to get her to eat but nothing sticks. She's losing weight too fast. I...I think we're losing her, Erin," Victoria sobs.

These few words stir something in me. Fire replaces my fear. I will not lose my soulmate.

Turning to face Amelia, the answer hits me. I know what I have to do. I couldn't explain how I know what I'm about to do is the right thing, and I'm sure the Loch family will protest, but tough shit.

"Can you leave us?"

Lucille starts to speak, but Harlan glares at her. I turn to Victoria once again.

"Please, Victoria."

She searches my eyes for a few seconds before agreeing. Lucille is ushered out under protest.

As soon as the door closes, I descend on Amelia. "Forgive me, my love."

Drawing back the sleeve of my top, I bite my wrist. Warm blood drips from the puncture wounds. Opening Amelia's mouth with my other hand, I allow the blood to drip until it's pooling at the back of her throat. Forcing her jaw shut, I pinch her nose. The action causes her to swallow.

Licking the wounds, I watch as they close. We're not in Kansas anymore, Toto. Shit is changing. Ignoring the usual questions banging around my head, I lean down and kiss her. My forehead connects to hers and I try again to reach her.

My heart blooms as I hear her voice calling my name. In the depths of our minds, we search for each other. The moment I mentally feel her soul in proximity to mine, I draw her in. Gold and blue light illuminates my mind's eye, and I know I have Amelia back.

Pulling back my head, I stare until I see her eyes flicker. Her gorgeous black eyes focus on me, and I see the light return.

"I'm so sorry," I cry.

Amelia lifts a shaky hand, cupping my face. "Please don't leave me again." Her voice is raspy, which kills me a little more.

"I'm sorry, baby." The floodgates open and I sob on her chest for what seems like hours. Obviously it's not, but by the time I've finished, her bedsheet is soaked.

"Amelia?" Victoria's voice echoes across the room. Moving, I give them some space. Harlan follows quickly behind, dropping to the bed and embracing his daughter.

I watch them hold each other, and I feel so lost. Amelia is my life, and yet, I feel the changes that are happening to me are pulling me away from her.

"Erin love, come here." Amelia calls quietly.

Stepping forward, I take her hand.

"You are not being pulled from me. You are changing, and I'm changing with you."

"Amelia, I scared you."

"No!"

"Amelia, I saw your face." Shaking my head, I can't look in her eyes any longer, not with the shame I feel weighing so heavily.

"I wasn't scared, but shocked, and not for the reason you think."

"Maybe this can wait a little while," Victoria interjects. "Amelia, we need to get some Red into you."

"Yes, let's talk later." I want to avoid this conversation for as long as possible. I know Amelia is going to say what she thinks I need to hear. My mind wanders to Jordan and Chris. Shit, where the fuck are they?

"She's here?" Amelia asks.

"Who's here?" Harlan asks.

"The one who bit Erin."

I need to stop this runaway train before we end up with a disaster.

"I need you all to listen. Actually, Amelia, I need you to listen first."

If I want the Lochs to understand, I need to go over everything that happened from the moment I left to now—with Amelia.

Opening my mind, I give her everything. She sits silently, looking at me, and takes in what I've found out. Harlan and Victoria sit patiently, knowing what we're doing.

In the end, Amelia blows out a breath. "Wow, okay."

"Can you share with us?" Harlan asks. Amelia glances at me.

"Okay, I need you to meet some people and not react."

They nod. Accessing the tenuous link between me and Jordan, I call for her, hoping it works that way. I nearly shit myself when Chris and Jordan drop from the fucking ceiling.

"Are you shitting me?" I hiss.

"We didn't exactly have anywhere else to hide." Chris grins. "Plus, the ceilings in this place are ridiculous. Have you seen how high they are?"

"Not to mention vaulted," Jordan tacks on.

I stare at them both in disbelief. "The *ceiling*!"

"Why not? It worked," Jordan asks.

"Because... I don't know."

"Erin, who are these two?"

"Fallen vampires." Chris smiles. Victoria and Harlan shoot to their feet in alarm.

"They're not Fallen. Well, not anymore."

Amelia sits up. "Mother, relax. Erin is telling the truth. They were Fallen but—"

"Erin saved us," Jordan announces.

Two pairs of dark eyes shoot toward me. "Erin?"

I nod. "It's true. The changes I've been going through. It's led to this. My bite changes them."

"Your bite?" Harlan is looking between me and them. Jordan stands straight, almost defiantly.

"Yes. Well, my blood or something. We're not sure. Jordan bit me and that worked, but when she took me to Chris, I knew the chemicals in my teeth were the answer."

Victoria looks like she's about to ask a barrage of questions. I hold my hand up to halt her.

"I have no idea how it's possible, and we can't go to the doctor."

Harlan takes a step closer to Chris, observing him. "Why not?"

"That's a longer conversation. Amelia needs to eat and rest and then we need to talk, seriously. Until then, no one can know we're here. Lucille needs to keep quiet, too."

"I'll talk to her," Victoria answers. I love how they take what I say and run with it, even though I know they are desperate for answers.

"Where is Dr. Mendhi?" Chris grinds out. The hatred the two vampires feel for the man seeps out of every pore.

"Asleep, I presume," Harlan says, returning to Amelia's side.

"He can't know we're here." I say with urgency.

If he suspects I've been in contact with the Fallen, I don't know what he'll do. I'd rather be cautious when it comes to him.

Harlan takes Amelia's hand. "He checks on Amelia regularly. It will seem strange if we stop him."

"Then we need to hide. Jordan, Chris, I suggest you leave the castle. Find a safe place and wait for me to call you."

"Okay. I'll take Chris to the place I stayed before. I should be able to hear you."

Noticing Amelia's flash of irritation, I know I need to explain about the connection I have with Jordan and Chris. But it will have to wait a little longer.

Leaning down, I kiss her hair. "Amelia, we need to come up with a story of how you're awake."

"No explanation is better," Victoria says. "Leave it a mystery. Just another one for the doctor to figure out."

"We'll leave you for the night." Harlan kisses Amelia. "Erin, where will you stay?"

"The castle is big enough for me to hide. Failing that, I'll crawl under the bed."

I'm not even joking.

"Maybe just nip into another room." Victoria smiles. "Dr. Mendhi visits at eight and then midday. He's like clockwork."

"Thank you."

We bid Harlan and Victoria good night. Sitting, facing Amelia, I lean in and kiss her deeply. God, how I've missed her. Our minds connect as we sink into each other. But then I feel the poke of another mind trying to listen in. Before I can reproach Jordan, Amelia lets out a growl, so low and threatening I gasp. My eyes whip open and see she is staring at Jordan with murder in her eyes. This is not the Amelia I know.

"Baby," I say, hoping to snap her attention back to me. It doesn't work. My gaze snaps to Jordan, who has gone white as a sheet.

"I'm sorry," Jordan gasps. "Please."

"Amelia," I scream in my head. This time it works, and she drops her death stare, turning back to me.

"I told you, I'm changing with you, Erin."

Fourteen

"Guys, can you leave us?"

What did Amelia mean, she was changing too? Jordan and Chris slip out of the bedroom silently. Just for a moment, I needed to look at Amelia. Trace her beautiful face with my fingers. I've missed her so much, and we haven't even been apart for that long.

"I'm okay now, my love."

Her voice still sounds raspy and upon hearing it, I close my eyes, consumed with guilt. Will it ever leave me? Do I deserve to be forgiven? No, I've made such a mess of everything and I can't actually think why.

I never thought I'd ever leave Amelia, not for anything. But I did. I've told myself that I left to keep

Amelia safe, but deep down I knew she'd get hurt by my absence.

"I'm so—"

"Please stop apologizing. It's done. But we do need to talk."

I sigh and nod, squeezing her hand.

"I wasn't lying earlier, Erin. When you bit me, I wasn't scared of you. I could never fear you."

"Amelia, you shut me out of your mind, and I saw your face."

"I was stunned at what I felt when you bit me."

"I attacked you."

"No, you didn't. You followed your instincts."

"Some fucking instincts," I scoff.

"Erin, my love, you need to listen. All the things that have been happening between us. The connection growing stronger, our ability to see each other's memories. There is a reason it's happening. I can't explain it. I wish I could."

"What does that have to do with—"

"You are changing. Your teeth are vampiric. You are hearing the cries of the Fallen. When you bit me, I felt the change start almost immediately."

"What change? I don't understand."

"I feel stronger. I know I look weak now, but as soon as I'm back to full health, you will notice the difference. My hearing and eyesight are far more enhanced than before."

"Like Chris and Jordan," I mutter.

"Mmmm."

Oh, Amelia is not happy about Jordan.

"Baby, we're connected to them. Both of us."

"Oh, I know. How do you think I sensed Jordan trying to snoop?"

"I think you scared the shit out of her with that growl. You kind of scared me."

"That's what I'm telling you. I feel powerful. I know my true purpose is to protect you."

"You've always protected me."

"No, it's different. I feel it in my very essence that... I don't know how to explain."

"We need to figure this out, Amelia. I feel like I'm going crazy. Jordan keeps calling me 'the key,' which is getting really old."

"Well, you did the impossible, my love."

"Maybe, but do you really believe I'm some ancient prophecy come to life?"

"We need to talk to Barty."

"We need to be careful. How are we going to do anything with Dr. Mendhi hanging around?"

"He needs to think everything is back to normal."

"You want him to know I'm back?"

"Yes, but he needs to see you return. Tomorrow, drive up to the castle as if you were coming back. We can spin the fact you freaked out over everything changing. It's plausible."

"It's true." I laugh.

"Erin, you're a human that found out vampires exist. Then you fell in love with one, agreed to get married, and then started turning into one spontaneously. I think you're due for a freak out."

"Well, when you put it like that."

We spend a few seconds smiling at each other.

"I love you, Amelia. With all that I am. I swear to whoever is out there, I'll never leave you again."

"Good. Now why don't you climb into bed and get some rest?"

"What about the doctor?"

"I'll set an alarm. We'll have you out of here well before he comes calling."

As soon as I feel Amelia curl herself around me, my body relaxes. I'm out like a light in seconds.

Moonlight is still shining through the window when Amelia nudges me awake. I grumble, because it's still the ass crack of dawn and all I want to do is stay wrapped up in Amelia.

"Love, it's time."

"Mmm, five more minutes."

Amelia's quiet chuckle sends shivers down my spine. Maybe we could spend those five minutes doing something else. And then it hits me like a truck. Amelia has only been conscious for a few hours. She needs rest. Because of *me*.

Reluctantly, I slip out of bed and dress. Amelia remains lying down, watching my every move. She already looks a lot better. Her color has improved drastically. We need to get some weight back on her, though.

"Okay, I'll see you in a couple of hours." I kiss her soundly. We agree Amelia should remain 'unconscious' until I arrive there to save the day. The notion makes me want to vomit. I'm no fucking savior.

Jordan and Chris wait for me in the kitchen. This connection thing comes in handy sometimes. Sneaking out leaves me feeling hollow. I don't want to be away from Amelia for a second, but we don't have much choice.

Jordan takes me to an abandoned cottage on the castle's estate. "Here, home sweet home." She grins.

"This is where you stayed?"

"Yup. It's rainproof, so that's good enough for me."

In the corner is a camping stove.

"Want some coffee?" Chris asks. My eyes lighting up makes him smile. "I'll take that as a yes."

We sit in silence for a little while. This is as good a time as any to find out a little more about my two new *friends*? Is that what they are?

"So, last night," I begin. "Jordan, you were out of line trying to get into our heads."

She holds up her hands. "I know. I'm sorry. I was curious. But trust me, I won't do it again."

"Be sure not to. What did Amelia say?"

Even though I heard the growl from hell, I'm guessing Amelia used the link to warn Jordan off.

"I—" She shakes her head. "Nothing, she said nothing."

I raise my eyebrows. She's lying out her ass. "Jordan, come on."

"I'm not lying. She didn't *say* anything."

"Meaning?"

"She showed me what would happen if I tried that again." Jordan visibly swallows deeply. "I don't want to talk about it, if that's cool. Just know, I won't do it again."

We fall silent again, but this time Jordan looks lost in thought. Or maybe the memory of whatever the hell Amelia showed her. Another cup of coffee and the time has come. Chris and Jordan will wait in the cottage until we figure out what to do about the doctor.

"Will you two be okay?"

"Of course. Don't worry." Chris is quick to reassure. I'm overwhelmed with the urge to hug them both. So I do. We've been through some stuff, and although our relationship is strange, I feel closer to them.

I order a taxi to take me from the entrance to the castle to the front door. If the driver thinks it's an odd request, he doesn't say. I tip him well, and he smiles. Probably thinks I'm some nutty American tourist too bone idle to walk up a driveway.

With a few deep breaths, I ready myself for the performance. Barty answers the door with a huge smile and a bone-crushing hug. I wonder if Victoria and Harlan let Barty and Anya in on the plan?

"Welcome back."

"Thanks," I mutter into his sweater.

"Are you ready for this?" he asks, answering my previous question.

I nod and then everything unfolds. Anya greets me before rushing off to tell the Lochs I'm back. We go through an entire performance before I'm whisked to Amelia, who is lying prone and unconscious. I mentally tell her I'm here and I love her. I can't repeat what she says back. Our time apart has had an effect on her libido, in a big way.

I can also feel the strength she alluded to yesterday. Everything about her is radiating power, even though she's supposed to be suffering from my absence. We need to get this over and done with before the doctor sees just how well Amelia is looking.

I go through the speech of needing to be with Amelia alone. The family plays their part well. I still haven't seen the doctor yet, but I'm assured he knows I'm back. As soon as the door shuts behind the last Loch, Amelia opens her eyes, smiling widely.

"Hey, long time no see," she jokes. I roll my eyes. Sometimes the tall, mysterious Amelia Loch can be a real dork.

"Hey, baby," I coo, leaning down to kiss her. We spend a long time reacquainting our lips.

"Mmmm, we need to do more of this." Amelia's hand wanders to my ass. I know this move.

"Amelia Loch," I chastise with a grin. "Now is not the time. We still have a performance to get through."

"Later?" she murmurs in my hair. Her lips suddenly on my neck, nipping.

"Christ," I hiss, because I am seconds away from forgetting about everything and letting her fuck me silly. "Amelia," I growl.

"Sorry."

Yeah, she sure as shit doesn't look sorry.

"Let's get this done and I promise tonight we will make up for lost time."

Amelia scoots back down the bed, getting herself into position. She gives me a nod and I take over. Rushing to the bedroom door, I shout for the doctor. Of course, the family follows, which is fine. It needs to be realistic.

"Amelia?" Dr. Mendhi says, flashing a light in her bleary eyes. She's a fantastic actress. "Do you know where you are?"

"E-erin," she croaks. I have to suppress a giggle.

"I'm here, honey, I'm here." I sit beside her, whispering loving things in her ear as the doctor takes her vitals, asking questions now and then.

"I'm satisfied she's okay. I imagine with your return her health will rapidly improve."

"Thank you, doctor."

The false pleasantries leave a nasty taste in my mouth. I respected this man once. I put faith in him. Now, all I can hear are Chris's pleas for help. The doctor did that to him. Even if Chris was a Fallen, Dr. Mendhi extended his torture.

"Take it easy, Amelia, and drink plenty. You already look better. It's remarkable."

"I will," Amelia replies, skipping the last part of his sentence.

"Erin, could we talk? I think it wise I check you over. Have you had any other surprises? Are your teeth—"

"Still pointy?"

Dr. Mendhi smiles. "Yes, are they still pointy?"

"Yes, but like before drinking Red stops them from suddenly popping out."

"You had Red with you?"

Shit, of course I didn't take Red with me when I ran away.

"Barty had a bottle in the car I took, fortunately."

Nice save.

"Interesting."

"Have you any theories?" Victoria asks, saving me from having to make any more shit up.

"Honestly, I'm a bit stumped. I can safely say that you're the first human to change spontaneously."

"So, you think I'm definitely becoming a vampire?"

"Erin, I'd say you *are* a vampire. May I take some blood to confirm?"

"Sure."

Of course I'm a vampire now. Everything is pointing to that. I suppose I'm finding it hard to let go of my humanity. My parents come to mind and I instantly feel sad. They're never going to understand this.

Amelia caresses my hand, her eyes full of love and understanding. Dr. Mendhi takes my blood and bids us goodbye. No doubt he's off to his portable lab.

"Harlan, ask Barty to make sure Mendhi stays away from the room for a while," Victoria instructs.

The entire family sits silently until Harlan returns.

"Okay, care to tell us what the hell is going on," Laurence booms.

"Keep your voice down," Victoria hisses, leaving her eldest well and truly chastised.

So, Victoria and Harlan informed the siblings that I was coming back, but they haven't received a complete update. Great. I have to go over everything again. And then something sparks in my mind. I see Amelia side-eye me with a questioning look.

It's another one of those things where I can't explain how I know I can do something. It just is. Standing, I look each Loch in the eye before closing my own. Their minds come into sharp focus, and I unleash the last few days on them. There are several gasps as they realize I'm able to connect with them, but eventually they settle and allow me to tell the story.

Fifteen

"Whoa," Lucas breathes. "That was insane."

"I second that," Aliah huffs.

"You were in my head!" Jacob states.

Okay, so the Loch children are more thrown by the fact I can connect with them rather than the story I told. Maybe it's a shock thing?

"You still shouldn't have fucking left," Lucille spits.

"I get it, Luce, okay, I get it. I fucked up, and I hurt Amelia. Trust me when I tell you I will never forgive myself, so you can lay off!"

"Lucille," Amelia warns. "I appreciate you looking out for me, but enough."

"Amelia..." I begin.

"No, Erin. None of us know what you've been going through. And quite frankly, you've handled everything over the last few years like a rockstar. I will not begrudge you a freak out. You came back, and that's all that matters."

"Amelia's right," Marcus adds. "Lucille, think about everything you've just heard. Is there any wonder she panicked?"

I look at the floor. I can feel tears prick my eyes, and I don't want Lucille to see how upset I am. In a flash, Amelia is by my side. Another wave of surprises echoes through the family.

"Jesus, Amelia." Maria chuckles. "How the—"

"I told you, I'm changing. Whatever is happening to Erin is affecting me, too. I'm stronger, faster, and...well, other things I'm not ready to discuss."

"But what does this mean?" Victoria asks.

"We need Barty. His savior queen thing might sound a bit out there, but it's the closest thing we have to an explanation."

I scoff, "Seriously?"

"Erin, you can save the Fallen and have suddenly gone from human to vampire. I think it's time we opened our minds to the fact that this goes beyond science."

165

"And what about the council?" Harlan asks. "We need to tell Mohan."

"I agree," Laurence adds.

"Until we know he's one hundred percent not in the know about the doctor's true working habits, it's not safe," Amelia replies.

"I trust him." My heart tells me Mohan is a good man.

"Me too," Harlan nods.

"Let's wait until we're back in the States," Victoria begins. "Now we know Erin isn't in danger. We should go home. Mendhi will go back to his lab—"

"Where he'll continue to hurt vampires," Aliah interjects.

"Yes, but also where we can monitor him. We need to be out from under his watchful eye. There is no reason he would need to be at the house, unless called upon. Same goes for the council. Being shacked up under one roof is dangerous, especially if there are unknown parties involved."

"Your mother is right. Amelia, we should go home."

"And what about Jordan and Chris?" I ask because there is no way I'm leaving them on their own.

"I'll get them stateside. I promise," Harlan replies.

"If you do that, I have a place for them to go."

Amelia's head whips to me when she hears the idea I've come up with to keep the two vampires safe.

"Erin? You can't!"

"Yes, I can, and you need to trust me."

"Erin can't what?" Lucille asks.

"Nothing. The less you all know of their whereabouts, the better."

Amelia is still boring holes into the side of my head, but I won't back down. I know where Jordan and Chris can hide. I just need time to get it all in place.

Victoria stands, placing hands on hips. "All right, it looks like we have a plan. I suggest we stay a couple of days to make it appear Amelia is resting up. Then we go home."

With everyone in agreement, the Lochs file out.

"Drink some Red, baby. You need to put some weight on."

"I'm already filling out, Erin."

"Just drink." I laugh. She's stubborn as a mule sometimes.

"Only if you drink, too. I don't want you worrying you're going to fang out."

If I didn't find her smirk so cute, I'd kick her ass for joking right now.

Leaning against the headboard, we drink our Red and just exist together. There has been so much going on that sitting here in silence is perfect. The Red soothes my throat and boosts my mood. I wonder if I'll still enjoy human food as much. Vampires still have a healthy appetite for regular non-blood sustenance, but with the differences between them and me becoming rather glaring, I fear that's one more facet that stands us apart.

"Try it and find out," Amelia says. I think back to the burger Jordan bought me. It tasted fine, but I wasn't exactly in the mood to eat then. I can't recall if I liked it or not.

"Maybe I could order a rare burger and see if it hits the spot."

"We still enjoy regular food. No reason you will suddenly take a dislike to it. Worst-case scenario, maybe it will just be a bit tasteless."

"I love a good burger. Do you think it's going to taste bland now?"

"Let's order you one and find out."

"Amelia, we have other things that are far more important than finding out if I still like burgers."

"Erin, I think we need a bit of normal for a few hours. Don't you?"

Taking the bottle of Red out of her hand, I set both of them on the bedside table.

"Hmmm, if normal is what you want, I can think of something else I want a lot more than food."

"Oh, Ms. Hanson, you naughty vampire!"

Why does Amelia calling me a naughty vampire send pleasure straight to my clit? Whatever, I'll explore that later.

Gently pushing Amelia down, I straddle her hips. "You're on bed rest, Ms. Loch. Why don't you let me do the work?"

"By all means." Her grin is wolfish, and her eyes are shining with mischief. God, I love this woman.

I start by removing her tank top. I know she's only wearing panties, so they won't take a second to discard. Oh, how I've missed her breasts. You'd think we'd been apart for months, the way my mouth waters at the mere memory of her nipples in my mouth.

Stroking my hand down her cheek, I lean forward and kiss her softly. I don't want fast and hard. This needs to be slow and loving. Our connection needs to be strengthened by the weight of our love.

Yep, it sounds super corny, but until you've felt the caress of another person's soul, and everything that means, it's not possible to understand. Loving Amelia

169

isn't just about saying the words or having the feelings. It's all-encompassing, it's every one of her cells being intricately linked with my own. It's her past, present, and future surrounding me, cocooning my mind until I can see nothing but her.

I shed my top, and briefly get off the bed to get rid of the rest of my clothes. Climbing back on, my hips slowly rock. Our pussies are perfectly aligned, and I can feel her clit rubbing oh so gently on my own.

Keeping the rhythm slow and sensual, I lean back down to take a nipple in my mouth. Amelia's body is visibly thin from the trauma she's endured. There's a voice in my head accusing me, shaming me, and I'm doing everything I can to block it out.

Amelia lifts my face with both hands. She remains silent but soothes my mind with one look. As much as I want to continue stimulating her breasts, I need to keep my eyes firmly on her. I need her to tell me it's all going to be okay.

As her hands drift down to my hips, encouraging me to press down and rock faster, my mind grows dark. This time, I'm not scared. I'm not craving Amelia's blood in the least. I don't want to bite her. This is something...different.

It's a familiar feeling. Our signature gold and blue lights swirl in the periphery of my mind and then I see. I see Amelia's memories again. We are deep in each other's minds as I rock harder and feel my clit tighten. My climax is building rapidly.

I'm faintly aware of my hands reaching up and caressing my breasts. I pinch my nipples, and Amelia moans. Her hips are meeting mine at every roll. We are going to hit the crescendo of our lovemaking together, which only makes the feeling grow exponentially.

"Oh Amelia, oh yes!"

"Erin, my love, don't stop."

Her word is my command and I surge forward, pressing down harder. Our screams echo through the room. I come to the vision of Amelia seeing me for the first time in her club.

The bedroom swims back into view. I'm still straddling Amelia, but my upper body is flat against her. Our chests rising rapidly together.

"I missed you."

Holding me close, Amelia traces my spine softly with her fingertips. "I missed you, my love."

"I have to say, seeing myself through your eyes is interesting."

"Same. It's bizarre having an orgasm whilst watching yourself in a memory, isn't it?"

"Hell, it's not the strangest thing we've faced." I chuckle.

"Not by a long shot."

Rolling off her, I tuck myself into her side, resting my head on her chest. "I wonder if our mind connection thingy will keep developing."

"Jeez, you sure use some technical terms, darling."

I jab her gently in the ribs. "Seriously. If I can suddenly connect to other people's minds, there's no limit to what we can do together. Don't you think?"

"What are you thinking?"

Shifting, I lean up on my elbow. Amelia's raven hair sprawls across her pillow, making her look like an ethereal goddess. Damn, she's gorgeous.

"Well, what if we can push the connection a little further? We're already able to see each other's memories. Do you think we could tap into the present? Like with our conversations, but through each other's eyes?"

"No idea, honey. I mean, anything's possible, right?"

"Do you want to try?"

"Now?"

I shrug. Since accessing the Loch family's minds, I'm eager to test my theory.

"If you want."

Amelia laughs. "Erin, you want to, so just tell me."

Grinning, I peck her on the nose. "Okay, I want to."

"How do you want to do this?"

"Close your eyes and open your mind completely to me."

Amelia immediately settles down, closing her eyes. She exhales deep and slow. It's a practice I recognize from her meditation sessions.

Resting my head close to hers so we're touching, I seek Amelia's mind. But this time I'm looking for more. Not her past or her thoughts, but her conscience. This could all be for nothing. I'm running on guesswork, but my gut tells me I'm on to something.

We lay silent as I explore. I have no idea how much time has passed, but eventually I come across what I'm looking for. Our minds are completely in sync. I have to disconnect from my consciousness and latch on to hers. Sounds far-fetched, but I know I'm right.

Suddenly Amelia's eyes open. She turns and looks at me. I can see my eyes are closed. Holy shit, it worked! I'm looking at myself in real time. Her hand reaches up and brushes a piece of hair from my face. I know my body felt it, but I feel disconnected. Aware, but nothing more.

Closing her eyes again, Amelia lays back down. My mind feels exhausted, and I can feel my grip slipping. Unable to hold on any longer, my eyes open with a gasp escaping my lips.

"Amelia," I call automatically.

"I'm here, love."

Turning my head, we gaze at each other, both scanning the other's face to make sure nothing is wrong.

"It worked, Erin."

I nod rapidly. "What did you feel?"

"I felt you there. You were present, but not overpowering. Like a passenger, along for the ride."

"I saw everything you saw!"

"I know." She chuckles.

"Why is this happening? Why now?"

"I wish I knew Erin, truly."

"I could kind of understand if I was thirty. That's the magic number, right?"

"For vampires, sure. But we always knew this wasn't an ordinary union."

"Barty and Anya didn't go through this."

"Which is why I want to explore Barty's theory."

Rolling my eyes, I sit up against the headboard. "Baby, I'm no ancient queen."

"Maybe not, but you have the ability of that queen. Whether that's because of evolution or some mystical legend, it doesn't matter, does it? We need to find out everything we can and adapt."

Sixteen

Our plans and warm comfort last for a grand total of four hours. A harassed-looking Lucille shatters the peace and quiet.

"We're leaving." Without further explanation, Lucille gathers our clothes, shoving them unceremoniously into our suitcases.

"Lucille, slow down. What's happened?"

Amelia is up and out of bed before I even have the chance to sit up and wrap the sheet around me. Her body is looking stronger by the second. The faint lines of muscle are etched on her body.

Shaking her head, Lucille doesn't even look up as she answers. "Ten more, Amelia."

"Ten more what?"

Halting Lucille in her tracks, Amelia steadies her sister.

"Lucille, ten more what?"

"Break outs. Ten more Fallen vampires have escaped."

I knew it would happen. That part isn't the surprise. It's the number that concerns me.

"How many Fallen are there?"

Mohan led us to believe there were only a few Fallen in existence. So far we are up to twelve, and I'm sure there are more.

"We don't know, Erin," Lucille bites.

"Lucille. Watch your tone," Amelia growls.

It's the growl that sends shivers down my spine because she is so goddamn intimidating when she does it. Even Lucille takes a step back.

"I won't warn you again, sister."

Silence descends. Lucille is used to fighting with Amelia, but even I know this is different. There is no sisterly banter. Amelia is seriously warning Lucille off.

"Sorry, Erin," Lucille concedes, her eyes wary.

We haven't got time for this. Lucille and I will be fine. Amelia's behavior is more of a concern, but even that needs to be put on the back burner.

"Let's move on. What's the new plan?"

"Mohan and the council, along with Dr. Mendhi, have already left."

Placing a calming hand on Amelia's rigid arm, I hope to snap her out of whatever rage fog she's currently living in.

"We need to find the vampires before the council, Amelia."

Taking in a long, deep breath, Amelia turns to me. "Don't worry, we'll find them."

"Father has chartered us a flight. We need to leave within the hour." Lucille continues packing our bags. Her posture is tight, and I see her shooting looks at Amelia.

"I need to talk to Barty and Anya."

Now I'm sure she's not going to beat up on Lucille, I peck Amelia on the lips and leave the room.

The castle is quiet, even though I know everyone is rushing around trying to get ready for our departure. Heading downstairs, I push open the door to Barty's library. Sitting on the two-seater couch, Barty and Anya are deep in discussion. "I'm sorry to interrupt."

They both turn to me. "Nonsense. Come in."

"You've heard?"

"Yes." Barty nods.

"I'll cut to the chase. Will you accompany us back to the States?"

If they're surprised, they don't show it. Maybe they were already considering it?

"I think that's wise," Barty answers seconds later. "Are you able to tell us what's really going on? I understand you needed to keep some things quiet, but—"

"Yes. Now the council and doctor are gone. It's safe."

That garners a surprised response.

"Why wouldn't it be safe with them around?" Anya asks.

I waste no time connecting to their minds. The moment I'm in, they share a look but allow me to continue. As with the Loch family, I take them through the events of the past few days.

"Yes," Barty begins once I disconnect. "We must come with you. I'll bring everything I have on the Salvator Regina. I also have friends in the U.S. who may prove helpful with research."

"We appreciate it, Barty. Can you be ready within the hour?"

"Yes, we'll be ready," Anya answers, already standing. "Don't worry, Erin," she continues, taking my hand. "We're with you."

It's an impressive thing to witness. Everyone in the castle is packed up and ready to go in under sixty minutes. Victoria takes the lead as expected. She's the matriarch and everyone is more than happy to let her do the hard work.

Several black SUVs line the front of the castle. Men in black suits help haul the mountain of luggage from the grand entry to the trunks. Harlan assures me that Jordan and Chris are already safely on the way to the U.S.

As always, Victoria and Harlan are the epitome of calm and collected. Surely, that's what two hundred years of living in this crazy world affords you. The ability to keep control in a crisis.

And it is a crisis. In my heart, I know the Fallen vampires will be executed if found. The doctor isn't going to risk the council uncovering his work. We have to get to them first. I have to help them.

Amelia's body snaking around me calms my racing thoughts. "We will find them, my love. I promise you."

Turning in her arms, I allow myself a second to unravel. On the outside, we look like two people sharing an intimate moment. In our minds, I'm breaking, and Amelia is once again being my pillar of support. Everything that has happened and what I think will happen finally overwhelms me. I'm scared for the Fallen, for my family, and finally, for myself.

"Sweetheart, it's time to go." Amelia's lips are close to my ear. Her voice soothes me, bringing me out from the dark cloud currently running rampant in my head.

Unlike the last time the Loch brood traveled together, there is silence. No quips or teasing. The siblings are in a world of their own. Lucille has positioned herself furthest away from Amelia and me. I have a suspicion it has nothing to do with her ire at me, but Amelia's display of anger in our bedroom earlier.

"Ask," Amelia mutters.

"I've never seen you react like that, honey. This anger that radiates off you when you believe I'm being threatened is new."

"It's since you bit me."

The one thing I can count on is Amelia always telling me the truth.

"When I said my purpose is to protect you, I'm not just saying words, Erin. Something has changed. I know

now, your purpose is to help the Fallen. It's a clarity I came to possess the moment you bit me. When I felt the change, it wasn't just physical. It was as if I could see our story, already written. I know what I have to do. I must be your champion, while you save them."

When I met Amelia, and she told me about herself, she was always the realist. She was the first to squash any unrealistic views I had about vampires. That fantasy humans had been fed angered her, and she had no qualms voicing her opinion. Now though, as I listen to her, I sense how far from that woman she is. Her views are changing. Is she really buying into some fantastical idea that I am some savior queen reborn?

"Amelia—"

"Erin, don't dismiss the idea that you are meant for more. I know you think I'm wrong, and you're worried, but please trust me. Everything is happening for a reason. For millennia, vampires have searched for a cure, a miracle that would prevent our brothers and sisters from falling into madness. We've failed repeatedly. But now, Erin, now we have you. You can't deny what you've seen and heard. There are two vampires that prove you have the gift of life. You literally saved them. If it's the label of being a savior queen that irritates you, ignore it. But don't ignore what you are, or what you're becoming."

"How are you this sure?"

Her belief is overwhelming.

"Look into my memory. Access the moment you bit me."

"I can't," I mumble. "I already tried."

I tried as soon as Amelia told me she was changing. The memory isn't there, or it's simply not for me to see.

"Then trust me. Open your mind. I know you can, Erin. You've been doing it from the moment you found out what I am. What you are now."

"This seems so much more. When I thought vampires were no different from humans, it was easy. But look at us. Jordan and Chris, too. We are different. You scoffed at the idea of fangs, but they're real. You're faster, stronger—"

"I still can't turn into a bat," she quips.

"Yet!"

"Okay, some things I ridiculed are becoming our new truth. But that doesn't mean we are becoming the monsters of legend, Erin. You are transforming into something that will heal our kind. That isn't written in human history, is it?"

"No, but—"

"You're scared, and I understand. I won't let anything happen to you or our family, my love. I wish you could feel how I do, but until that day, I'll have strength for us both. For now, try to concentrate your energy on resting. When we find those Fallen vampires, you're going to need your strength."

"And what of the doctor? What do we do about him?"

"We trust Mohan to deal with him."

"Mohan has been lying," I state confidently and a little too loudly.

"What do you mean?" Harlan asks from in front of us. All eyes are now on me. I can feel them from all directions.

"There were supposed to be a handful of Fallen. Clearly that's not the case, and I don't believe for one second Mohan wasn't aware. He's been hiding the severity of the problem. How many of those vampires mated with humans and we weren't told?"

"Why would he lie?" Victoria asks.

"To stop us from panicking," Marcus explains. "How do you think the vampire community would react to the knowledge that there were far more Fallen than expected?"

"Marcus is right," Aliyah adds. "From children, we are taught to fear the Fallen. Our entire existence up to the age of thirty is overshadowed by the possibility of becoming one. The only thing that keeps us calm is knowing there aren't that many around. Can you imagine the consequences if someone uncovered the truth? Especially when we are no closer to a cure."

"We need to establish if Mohan is simply keeping the truth to stop panic, or if he is in league with the doctor."

Harlan shakes his head. "I can't believe Mohan would condone Mendhi's unhinged practices. I just can't."

"Well, we need to find out," Lucille says. She is uncharacteristically quiet.

"How?" Maria asks.

"First, we get Jordan and Chris to safety," I say. "Then we need to get Mohan alone."

"To do what? We can ask him if he knows about the doctor, but he could be lying through his teeth," Laurence replies.

"Erin will know," Amelia supplies. She has the same idea as me. I need to access Mohan's memories. Maybe Amelia is the only one I can do that with, but it's worth a try.

"How?" Victoria asks. Her gaze is thoughtful. Amelia looks at me. She's leaving the decision up to me about how much I divulge.

"My ability to connect to the mind is developing," I say. "Amelia and I can access each other's memories."

"How long has this been possible?" Barty asks.

"Not long, but that's not all." Amelia gently places her hand on my thigh. "We've discovered I can become one with Amelia's mind in real time."

"What the hell does that mean?" Lucille shoots. At least she's sounding like herself again.

"I can reside in Amelia's consciousness temporarily. What she sees, I see."

"Have you ever heard of something like this, Barty?" Harlan asks.

"No. But that doesn't mean it hasn't happened before. I need to do more research. I'm sorry. I wish I could give you more."

Turning to me, Harlan takes a breath. "You think you can do the same with Mohan?"

"I don't know until I try."

"Well, we have several more hours in this tin can," Lucille chips in. "I suggest you practice."

Seventeen

I'd never been so happy as I was when we landed in LA. Hell, I was even happy to be sitting in outrageous traffic. However, even that paled in comparison to walking into our penthouse suite above Insomnia. It felt like a lifetime since we'd set foot in the place. The club was dark, which allowed us to get settled easily. The Lochs had taken most of the family back to the main house. Amelia and I, along with Barty and Anya, proceeded straight to the club from the airport.

Harlan assured me that Jordan and Chris would be waiting in the penthouse when we arrived. Amelia agreed to let them stay a night before taking them to my safe house.

A safe house, Amelia is not at all on board with, but one I know will be for the best.

"This is the guest room. Make yourselves at home. We'll order in tonight," I say to Anya, who looks exhausted. Barty and Amelia have already opened a bottle of whiskey. Jordan and Chris look uncomfortable and I feel on edge.

Amelia is still pissed at Jordan, and it's not like the penthouse is big enough to give everyone the space needed to cool down. Six adults are a bit much in one place, but we'll have to suffer through it for one night.

"Your home is lovely," Anya comments as she walks around inspecting bits and pieces.

"It's probably our favorite property. Don't get me wrong, we love our house. It's just the penthouse holds memories."

"Totally get that. Barty and I loved the barn we spent a few years living in, around, wow, must have been in the late seventeen hundreds. It was cold and damp, but we were together and really happy."

"Where was that?"

"Northern England. Just after the Union of The Crowns. We saw the birth of the Union Jack. Quite thrilling really."

"Have you been back since?"

"Oh, yes." Anya laughs. "Barty took me for an anniversary one year. Would you believe the building was still there? In fact, the current owner had it professionally remodeled. It's an Airbnb now."

"So you got to stay in it again?"

What a thing to have that kind of history.

"Yes, we stayed there for a week."

"I can't even imagine," I begin, and then freeze. I won't have to imagine, will I? I'm a vampire now and as far as I'm aware, now have immortality. I think.

Sensing my wandering thoughts, Amelia appears at the bedroom door. "We've got time to figure it out," she whispers. "How is the room, Anya?"

"Beautiful. Thank you for being such wonderful hosts."

"It's about time." Amelia chuckles. "It's no castle, but I think you'll enjoy it here."

"Oh, no doubt." Anya unzips her suitcase, reaching for the garment sitting on top. It's a gorgeous flapper dress that she probably bought in the 1920s. "Are we letting our hair down tonight, ladies?"

Amelia and I share a smirk.

"I think it's only fair," Anya continues. "We've had quite enough drama for a while. Let's take the night off. What do you say?"

"I'm in!" There is no question in my mind. We could all do with blowing off some steam and how lucky is it there happens to be a club just a few steps away.

"What about those two?" Amelia asks, twitching her head toward Jordan and Chris.

"They need to stay out of sight. We've no idea who is looking for them."

"I agree. Do you want to tell them, or should I?" Amelia's eyes twinkle in mischief. She's getting a kick out of unnerving Jordan.

"I'll talk to them. Would you relax? Jordan apologized already and won't try to do anything like it again."

All I get is a dissatisfied hum.

Rolling my eyes, I head toward the two vampires. Chris is looking so much better. His hair has been cut and his clothes replaced. Yes, he could do with a few more pounds being added to his still skeletal frame, but he has definitely put on a little weight.

When we first arrived in the penthouse, Jordan and Chris were lounging on the sofa, watching TV. The moment I saw them, my emotions came thick and fast. I all but sprinted to them, wrapping my arms tightly around their necks. I was so damn happy to see them.

"Hey guys."

"Hey," Chris mumbles through a mouthful of Cheetos.

"So, I have a plan."

"Amelia isn't happy about it," Jordan comments, looking in Amelia's direction. I follow her gaze and see Amelia's eyes boring into Jordan. Good Lord, what has got into her?

"Yes, well, that's for us to talk about. You'll stay here tonight, and then I'm going to take you to a friend's house. You'll be safe there."

Jordan narrows her eyes at me. "You're not one hundred percent sure about that, are you?"

"Yes, I am." Sort of. "I just need a little time to talk to this friend, and I'm sure it will all be great."

"She's a human, right?" Chris states.

Clearing my throat, I nod. "Yes, Mack is a human and a doctor. She doesn't know about vampires, but I plan to correct that tomorrow."

"And you think she's going to take it on the chin and then house two vampires without an issue?" Jordan raises her eyebrows in disbelief.

"She'll need a bit of time, but I trust her."

Jordan stares at me again, and I feel her probing my mind. I feel Amelia by my side instantly.

"What did I say?" she growls at Jordan.

Instead of shying away, something steely comes over her. "I said I wouldn't try to penetrate your minds. And I wasn't. However, the connection is there, Amelia, and I can tell when Erin is lying, or at least holding something back."

"Mack is my ex," I say, hoping to move us along. I really need to have a word with my wife-to-be. I get she wants to be my champion or whatever, but this thing with Jordan is just silly. A flash of hurt crosses Amelia's eyes. I've insulted her somehow. Great.

"Look, let me deal with it. But that's tomorrow. Tonight, you two need to stay up here. We'll order in, but then you two will be on your own for a while."

Jordan places her hands on her hips. She's in a combative mood.

"Why can't we come to the club? It's dark and loud. Who the hell would recognize us?"

"Do you really want to take the chance?" Barty asks from behind us.

"If it's really a big deal, I'll stay here, too."

My offer earns me a scowl from Amelia.

Chris shakes his head. "No, that's unnecessary. Go have fun. We've got a shitstorm ahead of us."

I look at Jordan, who casts her gaze to the floor. "Yeah, it's fine. Sorry."

∞

The club is thumping as we descend into the crowd. Heavy bass music shakes the floor. Anya is practically vibrating with excitement, which brings a smile to my face. Barty still looks like he's about to set off for a round of golf, but that's fine. As long as he's happy.

Amelia is sex on legs and she knows it. Dressed in all black, her hair hanging like a dark curtain over her pale skin, she is divine. I love the blood-red lipstick and dark eye makeup, too. Hell, I love everything about her. The instinct to drag her to bed was strong when she first stepped out of our bedroom. Always the one to make an entrance. Of course, she saw my thoughts and gave me that little grin that turns my panties into a useless barrier of wetness.

Kit and Claire are both working behind the bar tonight, as well as a new server. Claire beams at us as we approach. We share hugs and cheek kisses. Kit strolls over and does the same. The new girl is watching us from the corner of her eyes. Let me rephrase that. She's watching Amelia from the corner of her eye. In fact, she's watching every damn inch of my fiancée.

"Easy, tiger," Amelia laughs in my ear.

"Says you," I retort. "You don't hear me growling, do you?"

I'm still slightly annoyed by Amelia's new behavior. She's never been the type to get jealous or possessive.

"That's not fair," she mumbles, her gaze dropping to the drink in her hand. Once again, I seem to have hurt her.

Drawing in a breath, I lean in. "I'm sorry. That was uncalled for."

"It's fine," she says, dismissing my apology. "I'm going to talk to Claire about this month's stock."

And with that, she guides Claire by the elbow to the back room.

Shit, I've really upset her.

A tap on my shoulder pulls me from my thoughts. Turning, I come face to face with Mack.

"Hey, you're back. Where have you been?" she shouts.

"Oh, we took an impromptu vacation," I lie. "Actually, I'm really glad I bumped into you. Could I drop by tomorrow?"

"Yeah, sure. Everything okay?"

"Yeah, totally fine. We'll chat tomorrow."

Mack's eyes drift over my shoulder with a questioning stare. I turn to see Barty and Anya smiling at her widely. Jesus, they've been cooped up in that castle for way too long.

"Shit sorry, Mack, this is Anya and Barty. Friends from Ireland. They're staying with us for a little while."

"Nice to meet you," Mack yells. The music is getting louder by the second.

"We're going to dance," Anya calls. Barty shoots his drink, offering his hand to his wife. They stroll out and begin to move.

I can't label what they are doing as dancing. Laughter bursts from my chest as I continue to witness utter carnage. Barty and Anya could not give a flying fuck, though.

Anya's face is pure joy. I can hear her laughter over the bass. People are giving them a wide berth, which is wise. Both are quite liberal with their arm movements.

"Well, that's... Interesting." Mack smirks.

"It's certainly expressive." I laugh.

"Want to join them?" she asks. I hesitate for a second because I know Mack still has feelings for me. But if I get awkward, it'll just make things worse. Friends dance.

"Sure, let's go."

It's many songs later that I realize Amelia is still in the office. Reassured Barty and Anya are fine, I head to the back. Claire is behind the bar again, so why is Amelia still in the office?

Pushing open the door, I see her sitting at the desk, head in hands.

"Baby?"

Her head lifts and her eyes are blood red. Half-inch fangs protrude from her mouth. The sight is shocking, but I rein myself in.

"Amelia?"

"I'm fine, Erin. You don't have to be scared."

"I'm not. Concerned, sure!"

"I told you I was changing," she adds, almost defeated.

"Why didn't you tell me?"

"I did. You just didn't get to see the physical change."

"Why am I seeing it now?"

"I'm pissed."

Well, at least she gets straight to the heart of the matter.

"Um...okay. Why are you pissed?"

"Because you keep dismissing my protection as some childish jealousy," she growls. "Because I have a legitimate reason to warn off your little pet." Her tone is seething. "Jordan wants you. Her mind is like a fucking sieve. She can't stop the thoughts from pouring out, and I'm tired of listening to them."

Taking measured steps, I arrive by Amelia's side. Instantly dropping to my knees, I wrap my hand around her arm.

"You are my mate."

Slamming her fists on the table, Amelia's eyes penetrate my soul. "And yet, I'm sharing you with another!"

"You share me with no one. Amelia, you are mine, and I am yours. Bound for eternity. Nothing and no one will ever get in the way of that."

"I can handle your connection to the Fallen, Erin. Really, I can. I'm not a possessive asshole, you know that." I nod. "But Jordan is overstepping."

"Okay, I'll talk to her. She'll be out of the penthouse tomorrow. Then it's just you and me."

Amelia looks at me for a few seconds. "Would you think about cutting the connection?"

"I don't know how."

"If you found a way. Would you?"

"If that would make you feel better. Of course."

Dragging her palms across her face, Amelia shakes her head. "No. That's unfair for me to say. You have a connection with them for a reason. I'm sorry."

My heart aches. How could she possibly think I would... And then it dawns on me. I ran away, not necessarily with Jordan, but it ended up that way in the end. Amelia is feeling just as vulnerable with everything changing as I am. I've just been too selfish to see that she needs my reassurance like I needed hers. Amelia needs me to be her mate right now. Not the savior of souls, or whatever.

Eighteen

Barty and Anya closed the club down last night. They amassed quite the following, even getting several phone numbers of people who wanted to hang out with them again. Their flair for life was, or should I say is, outstanding. After all these years, they still love life.

They were still doing their version of a dance routine when they entered the penthouse. Safe to say, they entertained Jordan and Chris for a while. At one point, Anya was spinning Chris around like a ballerina. It was highly amusing.

Unfortunately, the tension between Amelia and me was still thick in the air when we went to bed. I'd tried to comfort her in the office, but she clearly needed some space.

I just found it hard that the space she needed was from me. Had I really neglected her feelings so badly? We'd never gone to bed fighting. I'm not even sure I could class it as a fight. I hurt Amelia. Which was so much worse than a stupid spat.

Normally, waking up alone wouldn't cause distress, but after last night, feeling the cold absence of Amelia stings. I know that once Jordan and Chris are safely hidden at Mack's, Amelia and I will have the room to talk properly.

I didn't realize Jordan's connection to me would have such an effect on my mate. Yes, I know Jordan would like more from me. She's not great at hiding her thoughts and feelings, but I never believed Amelia would take them to heart. We've dedicated our lives to each other. My soul is literally wrapped up in hers. How could she possibly feel Jordan is a threat?

The laughter of our house guests forces me out of bed. I'll deal with everything later. Right now, I need coffee and breakfast. Then I need to come up with a way to tell Mack about vampires without her passing out or thinking I've lost my mind. Or scaring the crap out of her. That one's possibly the closest to what will happen.

Jordan and Chris are roaring. Barty is recounting a story from the 1800s. He's very animated when he goes into storyteller mode. Anya is in the kitchen making eggs. Amelia is nowhere to be found. My heart sinks.

"She's on the balcony," Anya calls. Giving her a small smile, I suck in a breath and head outside.

"Hey, baby."

Amelia is leaning against the safety rail, her head pointing to the sky. The sun is shining on her, making those raven locks shine. She still takes my breath away.

"Morning, my love." She turns to me and smiles. Some of the anxiety I've been carrying since last night fades. Walking up to her, I take her face in my hands and look into her eyes.

"I love you, Amelia Loch. More than life. And I'm so very sorry I haven't been there for you, like you are there for me."

Amelia shakes her head, but I hold her still.

"Amelia, please let me say this."

"Okay," she mumbles through squashed cheeks.

"I'm so used to you being the rock. My rock. When all these changes started happening, I only saw my fear and anxiety. I'll be honest, it didn't even occur to me you may be struggling. You're always so strong. But that was an asshole thing for me to do. You told me the changes were affecting you, too. Hell, I saw them with my own eyes. Even so, I could only focus on what was happening to me."

"It's been a lot for you, Erin."

"And for you, too. This is new for all of us. I neglected to see how you were feeling and for that, I'm truly sorry."

"It's okay."

"No, it's not, but hopefully it will be. I intend to talk to Jordan."

"I need you to understand. I'm not just being a jealous bitch."

"I know. Once again, what I failed to see is how unique this situation is. When we mate, our connection is sacred."

Amelia closes her eyes and exhales. She's relieved I'm finally understanding. "It is."

"And for us, another has violated that sacred connection. We were never meant to share a bond with any other, and yet we are and probably will continue to do so."

"I can handle the connection. But—"

"Interfering with our bond is something different."

"It's unheard of. A vampire's bond is more precious than anything. Jordan may have been a Fallen, but that wasn't always the case. She knows what the bond means. And yet, she—"

"I know. I *will* talk to her. And, if after that she still pushes the limits, I will find a way to sever our connection. Nothing, and no one, means more to me than you. Our bond is a treasure worth more than all the gold on this pla—"

Amelia's lips cut my last words off. I cling to her as she owns my mouth. God, I want to climb her like a tree. My core ignites immediately, and my body takes over from my brain.

Grabbing the front of her shirt, I drag her backward to the sun lounger. Amelia's body lays over me fully, her weight a delicious sensation ramping up my need. Wrapping my legs around her waist, I use my feet to draw her closer. My clit is throbbing as her pelvis settles between my legs.

Throwing my head back, I encourage her to lick and kiss my neck. Her hips roll deeply, and I'm close to coming. It's ridiculous how turned on she gets me in such a short time.

"Oh, baby," I gasp.

"Hey ladies, we're— Oh, sorry!" Barty's voice is like a bucket of cold water. I hear the balcony door slide shut. Amelia buries her head in my neck and laughs. My face is flushed, both in embarrassment and lust. Looking over, I see Barty has also drawn the voile curtains across to give us privacy. My laughter soon catches up with Amelia's.

Popping her head up, Amelia's eyes twinkle in amusement. "Um...do you think we've scarred him?"

"Highly unlikely." I chuckle. "It's safe to say Barty and Anya have probably had their fair share of embarrassing encounters."

"I think we're going to have to save this for later."

If that's the case, she needs to stop nuzzling my neck.

"Then you need to move, because I'm about three seconds away from taking what I want."

"Ms. Hanson. You naughty—"

"Vampire?" I wink.

"Yes. Very naughty. Are you sure you don't want a quickie?" Amelia licks her lips while staring at mine. Her hips deliberately jerk forward, putting pressure on my clit.

I'm utterly powerless.

"Make me come."

$$\infty$$

Jordan wouldn't look us in the eyes when we came back inside. Anya winked at me, and Barty tried to bro out with

Amelia by going in for a high five. That earned him a jab in the ribs from his wife.

"Okay, I'm going to grab a shower and then we'll head out. Can you guys be ready to go in half an hour?"

"Sure," Chris calls from in front of the TV. Jordan nods. That's good enough for me.

Amelia follows me upstairs with a grin. Her appetite is far from sated. Before she can follow me into the bathroom, I plant my palm firmly on her chest.

"This is a no-go zone for you, Ms. Loch."

"But—"

"Nope. Later. If we start in here, it'll be evening by the time I get Chris and Jordan to Mack's."

Her pout is adorable and sexy. I lean in and bite her bottom lip.

"Later, baby."

"Fine," she grumbles with a smile.

"You can talk to me, though, from outside the shower."

"Can I ogle you?"

"As if I could stop you." I laugh.

Amelia sits on the empty surface by the sink as I undress and step under the shower. My mind goes blank for a few seconds, until it wanders back to last night, in the office.

"Baby?"

"Yeah?"

"Last night, you looked..."

"Different? Yeah, my fangs came out not long after you left. The eye thing shook me a little."

Amelia is so grounded, and calm when she speaks. Like the fact she has now grown large fangs and has blood-red eyes is not something to freak the fuck out about.

"You said you were pissed. Do you always change when upset?"

She takes a second to answer. "It seems to be one of the causes. I've been practicing though. Using meditation to calm myself. I've successfully changed three times when completely relaxed."

"Do you...do you crave anything?"

"Do you mean blood?"

"Yeah. I remember craving your blood. It took me over. Then, when I was away, I had an ache in my throat. I know it's thirst now."

"Nothing so far. Red tastes the same. I haven't had the urge to bite anything or anyone. I'm not sure what the purpose of my change is yet, but I'm certain there is one."

"Are you scared?"

"No."

Shutting the water off, I step out of the shower. Amelia looks completely at ease. Her gaze wanders my body, a smile pulling at her lips.

"God, you're stunning."

"Not so bad yourself, Ms. Loch."

Jumping down from the counter, Amelia takes me in her arms. I protest because I'm getting her clothes wet, but she ignores me and kisses me until my legs almost give way.

"You need to get dressed."

"Hmm, just another minute."

Her laugh ripples through my body, landing squarely in my heart. "Now, now, Erin. You have things to do today. Hop to it."

With a playful spank on my ass, Amelia takes a step back, allowing me to pass.

"You'll pay for that later," I huff, smiling.

"God, I hope so."

Dressing with Amelia watching me is something I love. I've never had a problem with my body. Even so, when

Amelia watches me, her eyes devouring my every curve, she makes me feel like the most beautiful and sexy woman in the world.

"I'm going to take Barty and Anya out today. Barty also wants to meet up with a friend of his."

"Please be careful. We don't know who's watching."

"I think we're safe, love. But of course, I won't take any chances."

"Once Jordan and Chris are safe, I think we need to contact Mohan. The faster we find out if he's on our side, the better."

"Agreed. All right, I'm going to leave you to it. A woman only has so much restraint, you know." Shooting me a wink, Amelia leaves.

I do a full body shake to rid myself of naughty thoughts. My head needs to be in the game. Applying makeup and dressing is the perfect way to let my mind wander into nothingness. If I continue to overthink how to tell Mack what I am, I'll just fuck it up. Look at where overthinking has got me so far.

Jordan and Chris are waiting in the kitchen when I come downstairs. Amelia, Barty, and Anya are already gone.

"Are you guys ready?"

"Sure this is the best plan?" Jordan asks.

"Yes. Mack has no ties to vampires. No one will think to look into her."

"And if she freaks out?" Chris asks.

"No idea." I laugh. "Guys, I'm winging this, okay. Mack is a good friend. I like to think she'll be able to get past her shock to help us. But until I speak to her, I really don't know."

"We need a backup plan." Jordan shoots.

She's irritable and I'm not sure if it's the situation or the thing with me and Amelia.

"No backup plan. This has to work. Let's go."

"Where does she live?" Chris asks.

"Outside the city. You'll be safe."

"Have a drink before we go," Jordan says, handing me a flask of Red. "It's been a while."

"Have you both had some?"

"Yeah, we're good." Chris picks up his jacket and walks to the door. "Let's get this show on the road."

Nineteen

Mack moved out of the city last year. Something to do with needing fresh air and space. I totally understand. I love the city, but it's always go, go, go. That's why Amelia and I bought a house further away. Sometimes, you just need some quiet.

Anyway, Mack now owns a lovely three-bedroom with a decent amount of land. Two-story, with painted shutters. I've tried to convince her to get a dog, but no luck yet.

It's the perfect hideout for Jordan and Chris. If I can get Mack onboard, that is. I'd sent a message as we left the penthouse, telling her I was on my way. I got an enthusiastic thumbs up in return. I wonder if she will still feel as enthusiastic in an hour?

Chris sat quietly in the back the entire ride. Jordan hummed to the radio but didn't make any real conversation. It was tense as hell.

"We're here," I announce the moment Mack's house comes into view. Chris cranes his neck to take a look.

Looking suitably impressed, Chris states the obvious. "Hey, it's nice."

"It's lovely. Mack has done a great job. Plus, she has a pool."

I look at Jordan, who is just staring out the window, keeping her opinion to herself.

"It's better than that shack in Ireland, that's for sure," Chris adds.

"Okay, you guys stay in the car. Let me get the hard bit out of the way first."

"Sure you don't want support?" Jordan asks, eyeing me closely.

"No. It's best I do this alone. I'll leave the keys with you."

Out of the corner of my eye, I notice Mack standing in her doorway, looking puzzled. I would too if my friend turned up with complete strangers at my house. Ha, wait until she finds out why they're really here.

It's now or never.

"Erin, hey." Mack embraces me tightly. "Who're your friends? They can come in, you know."

"Maybe later. Can we talk?"

I feel like I have a swarm of pissed-off ants in my stomach. Jesus, I thought my days of coming out were well and truly over.

Mack considers the car and then assesses me for a moment. "Sure."

Following close behind, I do my best to keep my heart rate normal. I really fucking hope she doesn't freak out.

"Coffee? Or is this a stronger drink kind of convo?"

"It might be." I smile.

Searching my face, Mack takes a seat at the kitchen island. "Okay, you're worrying me. What's going on? Is it Amelia? Are you okay?"

"She's fine, I'm fine. I'll explain. Um, just try to keep an open mind."

"I think I'm pretty open-minded, Erin. It can't be that bad."

I don't have scrolls of parchment to show her like Amelia used with me and I used with my parents. I plan to take a more direct approach. Which could backfire spectacularly.

Squeezing my eyes shut, I concentrate fully until I feel my teeth transform. I practiced discreetly in the car on the way over. It only took two attempts.

Opening my eyes, I reveal my fangs. It still makes me want to scoff and roll my eyes when I say that word. "Fangs" make everything feel... I don't know, fantastical. Not real, even though it is a reality.

Mack looks me in the eye and then her eyes dip lower. Her pupils dilate and her eyelids grow wide. I know she's trying to make sense of what she's seeing. I can almost see her brain fighting with itself.

"Erin?"

"Please don't be scared."

Please, please, please.

She raises her finger and simply points at my face. "What, they're—"

"Fangs. As in vampire fangs."

The smile I tack on might be a bit too much.

Mack takes a beat and then laughs hysterically. "Good one," she bellows.

Oh dear. I should have expected that.

Keeping a straight back and blank face, I touch her knee. "Mack, it's no joke."

"Stop. Come on, Erin. It's a weird time to be playing a prank, considering it's nowhere near Halloween. But whatever floats your boat."

She goes to stand, but I need her focused. Pulling her back down, I look at her with what I hope is a penetrating stare.

"Mack, listen."

She finally stops laughing and sees how serious my face is. Her smile turns into a frown. "Erin, vampires aren't real?"

"They are. Amelia—"

Mack holds up her hand to stop me from talking. Her palm is sweaty.

"You're telling me Amelia is a vampire?"

"Her whole family is, and now I am."

Mack opens her mouth and then slams it shut.

"Will you let me show you?"

"Show me?"

"Yeah. Um...it's a thing I can do."

So far, I'm just happy she hasn't tried to stake me with a wooden spoon or anything yet. We spend several more seconds looking at each other. I'm trying to convey calm and safety.

"What do you need to do?" she asks tentatively.

"Will you close your eyes?"

Another few seconds pass until Mack closes her eyes. Now, I've only ever connected to vampires. I have *no* clue if I can with Mack, or if she'll accept it without issue. But in order for her to fully understand, I need to go all the way back to when I first met Amelia.

Summoning all my strength, I focus solely on Mack. My consciousness seeks her like a homing device. I'm getting quite good at it, even if I say so myself. It takes only a second to see her light. I pull her toward me, and then, like a zap of electricity, we connect with a jolt.

Mack's mind is a hive of anxiety and fear. My voice echoes within, soothing. Eventually, I get her calm enough to show her a reel of memories. It's difficult to keep her calm, edit the memories—because she does not need to see some of the saucy ones—and show them to her in a way they make sense.

By the time I'm finished, my mind is jelly. I sever the link and let my head sink to the kitchen worktop. The cool surface eases the tension currently running across the front of my skull.

My vision is blurry, but other than that, I think I'm good. Lifting my head, I take in Mack, who is still sitting with her eyes closed. Oh fuck! Have I broken her?

Gripping her hand, I squeeze hard. "Mack?"

"Ow, fuck, Erin." Mack withdraws her crushed finders, shaking them out, staring daggers at me. "I kind of need my fingers intact."

"Sorry," I rush to say. "Are you okay?"

"Am I okay?" She taps her fingers on the work surface rhythmically. "Am. I. Okay?"

"Um, yeah."

Jesus, please don't have a brain injury.

"You're a vampire. Amelia and her family are vampires. There are crazy vampires that only you can save."

Yeah, that pretty much sums it up.

"Uh, yeah."

"Huh, okay. I need a drink. Um…could you put them away?"

My hands fly to my mouth to cover my teeth. Finally, I get them back to human-like standards. Mack has already sculled a shot of vodka. She's already pouring another.

Sitting quietly, I kind of wish she'd give me one, too. "Can I have a drink?"

Mack looks like she's forgotten I'm here. With a nod, she pours out another drink and hands it to me. I waste no time throwing it down my neck. I love the burn.

"Fuck Erin! Vampires!"

After Mack's fourth shot, I felt it necessary to take the bottle of vodka away. There is a time to get black-out drunk, but now isn't it. Mack scowled at me for a second, but then thankfully took the bottle of water I offered.

Three bottles later, Mack is a little less bleary-eyed. "So, your friends in the car, they're...you know."

"Yes. They are. They're the two I helped."

"Right, right! And they're here because, I'm guessing you need a place to hide them."

"Yes, I couldn't think of anywhere else, Mack."

"So if you didn't need my help, you'd never have told me?"

Fair question.

"I've wanted to tell you for the past two years, but come on, Mack. This is all so...out there."

"Yeah, you got that right."

Walking over to the couch, Mack is slumped in, I take a seat next to her.

"There was never a guarantee how you would take it if I told you. My parents are a good example."

"I'm sorry about them, Erin. I'm sure they'll come around."

"Hopefully, but I can't worry about that now. I have to help these people, Mack. And I know I'm being shitty by asking you to help."

"But you're still asking anyway, right?"

Sighing, I nod. "Jordan and Chris are good people. Chris has suffered for so long. I have to keep him safe now. He needs care and a place to unpack all the shit he experienced."

Standing, Mack paces the length of her living room. We moved from the kitchen when Mack got a bit wobbly. Whether that was from shock or the multiple vodka shots, I'm not sure.

"Of course I'll help. I... You're sure they, sorry, *you*, don't like human blood?"

Grinning, I fight the urge to mess with her. "I promise. We drink animal blood. Jordan and Chris have come prepared. They just need a safe place. You're in no danger, Mack. I swear."

"Jesus," she huffs. "This is not how I thought today would go. I'm still not sure if you're fucking with me."

"No fucking about, I promise. I know it's a hell of a lot to take in. Trust me, I know, and if you need anyone to talk to or have any questions, just call. Or ask Jordan and Chris."

"Fine. Yeah, okay, send them in."

"Sure?"

"Yes, before I change my mind and commit myself because I'm likely having a mental break."

Rolling my eyes playfully, I head to the front door. Chris is fast asleep in the backseat, and Jordan is moving her head to whatever beat she's listening to. Waving, I finally catch Jordan's attention. They both look wary as they approach the house.

"It's fine. Mack's cool." I soothe.

"How did you tell her?" Chris asks, his eyes wandering over my shoulder, scoping out the entryway.

"Whipped out the fangs." I laugh.

"Bold," Jordan comments. "And she didn't try to stab you or anything?"

"Nope. I was able to get through to her. Obviously she's still in a state of shock, but Mack's a doctor, and she's pretty awesome at adapting. That being said... Can you both rein in your speed and strength?"

"We're not going to freak her out. Don't worry." Chris pushes past me, quite happy to meet his new landlord.

Jordan and I follow behind. Chris walks straight up to Mack, holding out his hand.

"Hey, I'm Chris."

Mack looks at his hand, then up to his mouth, and then his eyes.

"Oh, I don't have cool teeth like Erin. Just the regular ones." He smiles.

We all see Mack visibly relax. She takes his offered hand and shakes it firmly. "I'm Mack. Welcome."

Pushing her forward slightly, I introduce Jordan. "And this is Jordan."

Mack stares, saying nothing. Her eyes are trained on Jordan's. Following her gaze, I see Jordan is just as frozen.

Um, okay...what's happening?

"Right, now introductions are out of the way. How about we have a coffee? I'll need to head back soon." I say, trying to break the atmosphere.

Chris is smirking, looking between Jordan and Mack.

"I think we could both leave and they wouldn't notice." He chuckles.

I think he's actually right.

"Mack," I all but bark. Mack jumps like I've just electrocuted her.

"Sure, yeah. What?"

Oh boy.

"Coffee." I repeat.

"Yes. Coffee. I'll make some."

Jordan still hasn't said anything, and she's still tracking Mack as she makes her way to the kitchen.

"Jordan?"

"Erin, it's her."

"Um...what's her?"

"Mack. I..."

Chris wanders over. "Erin, she's found her mate."

Twenty

Jesus fucking Christ!

I believe that's an appropriate response, right? Yes, definitely. Jordan is staring at Mack like she hung the moon. Chris is tittering to himself, looking back and forth between us all. Mack keeps on throwing glances at Jordan over her shoulder as she—for the fifth time—forgets what she's doing. Making coffee, that's what she's supposed to be doing.

"I need to tell her." Jordan suddenly gasps, her hand clutching her shirt. The desperation in the woman's eye is shocking.

"Whoa, Jordan, you can't just announce she's your mate," Chris reasons.

At least he's stopped laughing and is being helpful. Because frankly, I'm dumbfounded. Of all the times for this to happen, am I right?

"That poor woman has literally just found out her childhood nightmare exists and is standing in her kitchen. I think declaring your immortal love to her might be a bit much."

"But she needs to know. We're meant to be." The conviction in her voice is heart-wrenching.

Oh, brother.

"Jordan, Jordan!" Her eyes snap toward me, but she still looks unfocused. "I understand, believe me, I do, but you need to be patient. In fact, you need to talk to Amelia."

Yes, that's a plan.

"Amelia, why?"

"Because if anyone knows what you're feeling, it's her. She mated with a human too, remember."

And she suffered.

No, we can't let Jordan go through what Amelia did.

"Right, yeah." Jordan's eyes have already drifted back to Mack.

Okay, time to take action. "Mack, slight change of plan. I need to take Jordan with me for a few hours. Are you okay with Chris staying?"

Mack looks at Jordan, her eyes searching. Does she feel the same way? Wowzer, this is more than I bargained for today.

"Um...sure."

"Great, okay, sorry we can't stay for coffee. We'll be back later."

I have to physically remove Jordan from Mack's kitchen. Once wrangled into the car, Jordan watches Mack's house disappear behind us. Is this what Amelia was like when she met me? The thought brings a little smile to my face. Was she all googly-eyed every time she saw me?

I really hope Amelia is home.

My prayers are answered. Amelia is making lunch as we walk in. Her open smiling face quickly turns sour at the sight of Jordan. No real surprise.

"There's been an unexpected development."

Amelia's eyebrows furrow. She looks at Jordan and then her eyes widen. "She's mated. With a human!"

"Hey, reading my thoughts is cheating."

I was sort of looking forward to telling her.

"I didn't. I can smell it."

Um, okay.

"Smell what?" Anya asks, slipping in from the balcony.

Amelia juts her head toward Jordan. "She's mated with a human." Taking a deep inhale through her nose, Amelia's eyes widen even further. "She's mated with Mack!"

"How are you doing that?"

Is this another new skill Amelia has gained since I bit her?

"No idea how I'm doing it. But I'm right, aren't I?"

Grinning, I nod. "Spot on, baby."

"Oh, wow." Anya approaches Jordan tentatively. "Yeah, she's way off in love land."

Jordan has this wistful look about her. I imagine she is picturing Mack in her kitchen and thinking she's the most beautiful thing she's ever seen.

"I'm thinking this whole falling in love with a human thing is about as rare as the Fallen." Amelia and Anya note my sarcasm.

It stands to reason, doesn't it? If we've been lied to regarding the true number of Fallen vampires. It's possible we've been fed a bunch of shit regarding how many of those Fallen mated with a human. A hideous thought settles in my mind. Would Mendhi go as far as experimenting on humans? Would he want to find out what made them different from other humans? Why their souls bonded—unsuccessfully, but still—with a vampire?

"I would never have believed it," Anya begins. "But yeah. I think it's more common than we believe."

"Does Mack know?" Amelia asks, her stare trained on Jordan. If I'm not mistaken, my beautiful wife-to-be is softening. I can see her empathy for Jordan emanating in pulses. Is she recalling how she felt when we bonded?

"No, but they definitely shared something. Jordan wanted to confess her undying love immediately, but—"

"Yeah, I get it. I'll talk to her." And just like that, Amelia sweeps in, taking Jordan by the arm, walking her to the balcony.

I watch them leave, hoping Amelia helps Jordan get through this. Should *I* talk to Mack? Hmm, maybe not. Jordan might not appreciate Mack's ex getting involved that much. I'll trust Amelia on this one, I think.

"Coffee, or whiskey?" Anya asks. I'm grateful for the break. My mind feels like it's playing *Tetris* with everything going on recently, and none of those fucking blocks will fit.

"Coffee, but I'll take a hard drink later. Where's Barty?"

"Meeting with his friend. I thought it best to leave them to it. They're quite happy nerding out, and there really is only so much I can handle. I wanted to check in with you, too. It's been a few days since we've had the chance to talk properly."

"You're sweet. I appreciate it."

"So? How are you?"

"Tired, confused, excited, irritated. All the above. There's just so much happening. My brain is struggling to keep up."

"Understandable. Any more changes?"

"No. Apart from my ability to reach other minds. That's still developing. For what purpose, I'm not sure."

Anya rubs her chin in thought. "Maybe so you can reach the Fallen. Not just the ones you saved, but the ones still suffering."

Huh, I hadn't thought of that.

"It would make sense, right?"

"Yeah, I suppose it would. For whatever reason, they've become aware of me. Jordan said it was like a light of hope passed through her, changing her thoughts. She said all she could think about was getting to me."

"Exactly, so let's presume the other Fallen are in the same boat. There are ten of them out there looking for you. Well, what if you could use your new skill to guide them safely?"

"But I don't know who I'm looking for. Normally I'm in front of the person. I know what light to look for."

"Light?" Anya sits at the table.

"When I'm looking for the connection, it comes to me as a light."

"And what happens when you find it? The light, I mean."

"I draw it in and then, it's like my mind wraps around it, causing us to link."

"Okay. Are the lights always the same for each person?"

"Similar, but not exact. It's hard to explain. There is always something unique about each light."

"Okay, think back to Jordan and Chris. Do they share any similarities?"

I see where Anya is heading. If the Fallen share a commonality, I might be able to single it out and find them. Calming my thoughts, I reach out to Chris and Jordan. I'm sure they can feel me, but I'm not trying to link up. I just need to see their lights.

Maybe it's because I've already connected with them before that I find them so easily. In the darkness and silence of my mind, I examine each light. I know the differences. I can feel them. I'm almost ready to give up when I finally

228

find what I'm looking for. Their lights are slightly dimmed at the heart. They've been irrevocably altered during their time as Fallen vampires. That's what I need to search for.

Bringing myself back to the room, I take several deep breaths. "I think I know what to look for."

"I knew you'd figure it out. Now what?"

"We need to talk to Mohan. Even if I find the Fallen, more will surface eventually. We need the council on our side, and Mendhi needs to be dealt with. We can't keep this cloak and dagger shit up. Not when we think there are far more Fallen vampires out there than expected. We need to do this right."

"Agreed." Anya stands and tugs me into an embrace. "I know you don't want to see yourself as a queen or savior, Erin. But you are special. Whatever the reason for your change, it's important. You are meant to do great things."

"It scares me."

I can't recall if that's the first time I've voiced it out loud, but that's it. The reason I can't get a grip on my current reality. I'm scared shitless. I was meant to be a regular old vampire. Well, that was the hope when I turned thirty, which is still months away. I wasn't supposed to be special to anyone but Amelia. Now I have this responsibility, and I'm not sure that I'm cut out for it.

"I'd be concerned if you weren't scared. But Erin, you aren't alone. Even if you discount the Loch family, plus me and Barty, who are in your corner, one hundred percent. You have Amelia. She is inherently bound to this, to you. Her physical and mental changes have a part to play. I'm positive."

"She told me she understands her purpose. That when I bit her, she became aware of her *true* purpose. To protect me."

Anya grips my shoulders. "I think it's more. My gut feeling tells me it's more."

"Like what?"

"If we're to go along with the theory that you are somehow this Salvator Regina, we should assume other parts of the legend may have merit."

"You know way more than me. We only covered the savior part last time."

"Okay, so according to Barty, the savior queen was a vampire who had special skills. She was like you. A human who bonded with a vampire and changed. She was real, not just a myth. The name Salvator Regina was given in a time of superstition. Anyone who was different received reverence or fear. According to the story, the queen was attacked by a Fallen. When bitten, the Fallen vampire suddenly changed. There were witnesses, and her legend was born."

"Sounds eerily similar."

"Exactly. If we look at it in today's age. The skills she had weren't sent from god, or obtained by magic. They're a product of biology, changing things up. Just how a human can be a musical savant, or have the ability to endure subzero temperatures without dying—"

"Who can do that?"

"Some guy called Wim. He's known as the Iceman. Anyway, You get my point. Evolution, biology, they like to throw us curve balls sometimes."

"I'm a curveball?"

"Yes. And I think Amelia is, too."

"Because of the legend?"

"Yes. In the story, the queen had a mate who had the ability to change humans."

"To vampires," I almost shriek?

"Yes. Erin, think about it. We know vampires can mate with humans. Except for me and yours truly, they've been unsuccessful. Now we know a Fallen vampire can be saved. Surely that means their human mates can be saved, too."

"Saved?"

"From living a mortal life without their mate. You remember the thought of living without Amelia, yes? How the idea that you might not change plagued your mind constantly."

"Of course I do."

"We are made to find our other halves, our missing piece of the puzzle. Our soulmates. If a vampire mates with a human, there has to be a way to change them, without relying on a hope they will change at thirty."

"But what about the sharing blood thing? Both you and I did that with our mates, and the bond took."

"That was before our mates turned thirty. What about the ones that passed their deadline and became Fallen?"

"I..."

I what? I have no idea if it's true. Does Amelia have the ability to change a human mate?

"It's possible." Amelia's voice echoes through the penthouse.

Twenty-One

"How's Jordan?" Anya pours Amelia a coffee. I'm desperate to know what Amelia said to Jordan, and my mate knows it, too.

"Thinking, digesting. Finding your mate is akin to having a sledgehammer hit you square in the chest. She just needs a little time."

Amelia pecks me on the lips before grabbing her coffee. She's so calm and poised. God, I want to ravish her.

"And what's the plan regarding Mack? We need to get Jordan back to safety, but I'm not taking her back if the first thing she does is propose to Mack."

I'm joking. Sort of.

"She understands the need to practice patience. I think now the initial shock has worn off. She's back to rational thinking."

"So, is it safe to take her back? I'm nervous about her being in the city. I wouldn't have brought her back if—"

"My love, you did the right thing. Jordan was overwhelmed and leaving her with Mack would not have gone well."

Peeking out to the balcony, Anya surveys Jordan for a second. "Erin can take her back then?"

"Actually, I'd like to take her if that's okay with you." Amelia wraps her arm around my waist, dipping her head to inhale my scent.

"You want to take Jordan to Mack's place?"

I'm just clarifying because I never thought I'd see the day Amelia would volunteer to take Jordan, a vampire known to have a crush on me, to my ex's house.

"Yes. I'd like to test a theory."

"The theory being?"

"That I am indeed meant to help humans become vampires."

"Whoa, we were just spit balling here. You can't go around biting humans, babe."

Amelia's laugh echoes through the penthouse. "Obviously not, Erin. I just need to see if there is a change in me when I'm near a human who's mated with a vamp."

"I think it's a good idea," Anya chimes in. "Just like you, Erin, Amelia will feel it instinctively if there is any truth to it."

"And what if she can't control herself?" I demand. "Amelia, I bit you because I couldn't control myself!"

"Yes, which is why I think Anya should come with me. Chris is there, too. I'll fill him in. Jordan is onboard."

"And what am I doing in all this?"

"You, my love, will meet with Mohan. You don't need me there to connect with him. Call Mother and arrange to meet at the house. That way, you'll have backup if you feel something is wrong."

Dropping my voice an octave, I lean up to Amelia's ear. "You're really sexy when you get commanding, FYI."

Her soft, gravelly chuckle makes my pulse race. When her voice gets all husky like that, I know she's turned on.

"Behave, Ms. Hanson. And be safe."

"You too, honey." The kiss that follows is tender and full of love. Anya finally clears her throat when we're no closer to ending it.

Anya picks up her purse. "Shall we go? The sooner Jordan is out of the city, the safer for all of us."

"You're right. Erin, let me know as soon as you're finished with Mohan. And please, promise me you won't try to call for the escaped vampires until we're all together."

"Cross my heart. I'll see you later."

Secure in the knowledge that Jordan is on her way to safety, I drain my coffee. The caffeine kicks me like a mule. Goddamn, Anya makes some good jet fuel. I type out a message to Victoria, letting her know I'm on my way.

Kit and Claire are setting up in the club. At some point, we need to fill Claire in on everything. She's been a wonderful friend throughout the years and the last thing I want is for her to worry about escaped vampires. Our community is still under the opinion that Fallen vampires equal chaos and death.

Waving them goodbye, I jump into the Aston Martin Harlan and Victoria gifted me last year. It seems their thing is to buy hella expensive presents for family, even those not related by blood.

I have to say, I'm not usually a gearhead. That's more Amelia and Victoria's vibe, but this car is one hundred percent outstanding. Just a tap of the pedal and off it shoots, stirring all kinds of adrenaline-fueled excitement.

At least the ride over takes my mind off what I'm about to attempt. Hopefully, Mohan is open to the idea of me sifting through his memories. I imagine he's going to be offended at first. I wish I could trust him on blind faith alone, but someone on the council is working in partnership with the doctor. I don't believe it's the Grand Master, but stranger things have happened.

As expected, the entire clan has assembled. Victoria meets me by the door.

"Erin honey, it's good to see you."

"You, too. Is everyone here?"

"Yes. I thought it best. Was I right?"

Nodding, I fill Victoria in on the plan. She laughs when I tell her about the slight hiccup with Jordan and Mack. I neglect to say anything about Amelia and her theory. That's for my mate to divulge if she so wishes.

We walk into the dining area, where the Lochs are sitting, waiting. Harlan stands. "Erin, I've called Mohan."

"Is he coming alone?"

"Yes, I told him the meeting was of the utmost discretion."

"Do you think you can do it?" Victoria asks, earning a few quizzical stares. I bring everyone up to speed. I'm not sure who knows what anymore.

"I'll try. I'm sure I can connect to him. It's accessing his memories that might take some work. If he's obliging, that might make it easier than fighting against his mind."

"The Grand Master will open his mind to you. I'm sure of it."

I hope Harlan's right. I don't want to disillusion my own soon-to-be father-in-law of his dear friend's character.

"Where's Amelia?" Lucille asks. Her tone is far more friendly than the last time we spoke.

"She wanted to take Jordan to the safe house."

"Really?" Lucille's surprise is warranted. It's not like Amelia didn't make her feelings toward Jordan known.

"Yes. There's been a development."

"Oh god. What now?" Lucas asks.

Mohan walks into the Loch family mansion thirty-four minutes later. His usual disposition is firmly in place, which relaxes me. We greet each other with a hug.

"How are you, my dear?"

The last time I saw Mohan was at the castle with brand-new fangs.

"I'm good. Thank you for asking."

"Wine, Mohan?" Harlan pours Victoria a drink before serving the Grand Master.

"Certainly. Now, may I ask what this secret meeting is about?"

I share a look with Victoria and Harlan. Here comes the tricky part.

"Mohan, there are things that need to be said. However, before I divulge this information, I need to...I need to be sure I—"

"*We* need to be sure," Victoria clarifies.

"Yes, *we* can trust you. Please don't be offended, you'll understand soon."

We spend a fraught few seconds watching Mohan weigh up his decision. He looks at each of us for a few seconds before settling his gaze on Harlan. Harlan, to his credit, doesn't flinch.

"Okay Erin, what do you need?"

"I've...um, found a way to...um, could you just close your eyes?"

Mohan slips his eyes shut, and I take a steadying breath. Blocking out all thought, I venture into my consciousness. The darkness is calm and welcoming. I see Mohan's light immediately. It's brighter than anything I have ever seen, but also welcoming. He is literally radiating warmth and safety. That's a good start.

Wrapping myself around his light, we connect easily. He doesn't flinch or fight it, making me wonder if he's done this before. The next part is a little trickier. I've only ever accessed Amelia's memories, and that was in the middle of an orgasm, so...

Mohan's mind soothes me. He's actively helping me. With renewed confidence, I continue until I find what I'm looking for. It's like a window opening, inviting me in to take a look around.

I have no idea how long I spend flipping through Mohan's memories. I mean, he has a lot. But, by the time I reach one from last week, I know he's safe. Mohan is the man we thought all along. Good, kind, and loyal to his people.

It's no wonder they vote him into office every fifty years. I witnessed how bravely he fought against vampires who wished to hurt the Fallen. How he won over the masses with humility and empathy. The man is a legend. Because of him, the vampire community found peace through democratic voting. It was he, who brokered a peace between the divided parties.

Mohan is the reason the human world remains ignorant of vampires. His leadership and wisdom forged a path for all other Grand Masters to follow. I have a whole new level of respect for him.

Relinquishing the link is easy, because once again I can feel the Grand Master aiding me. Victoria is behind me, supporting my upper body. We must have been standing for a while, because my legs are almost asleep.

Mohan gracefully takes a seat, rubbing his head. "Well, Erin, that was interesting."

"I'm sorry, Mohan, I needed to know."

"And you're satisfied?"

"Yes. Now we need your help."

The entire Loch clan jumps in to fill the Grand Master in on all the things that have transpired lately. I take the opportunity to update Amelia. I feel her elation and it helps.

"Here, drink this," Lucille whispers.

I take the wine and all but drain the glass in one fell swoop.

"I'm sorry, Erin."

Her sudden apology causes me to look at her. Lucille doesn't apologize. "It's fine."

"No, I was a bitch. But in my defense, I was scared. I just don't know how to deal with big emotions like that sometimes."

Wow, okay.

"You were right, though. I promised I wouldn't leave or hurt her, and I did."

"You got scared, too. And I understand why. I'm so—"

"No more apologies, yeah? We're okay?"

"Yeah, we're good. I missed talking to you."

It's true that we've become close over the past few years. Lucille is sharp corners and blunt words, but she's gooey on the inside and fiercely loyal to the ones she loves.

Mohan, clearing his throat, draws me back to the bigger conversation. "I... It's not often I find myself lost for words. But I am."

"We need to find out who is helping Mendhi."

"It can only be one of two people. Sabine, my aide, or Noah."

"Noah? Really? He's second only to you on the council, Mohan."

"A position I know he covets, Harlan."

"Enough to work with the doctor behind your back? And for what purpose?"

"On that, I couldn't tell you. Noah craves power."

"And Sabine?" Victoria asks.

I've only met the aide once. She's a mousy woman who hardly speaks.

"Sabine has been working closely with the doctor on my behalf. I find it unlikely she wouldn't find out what he's been doing."

"Erin, can you find out if either of them is guilty?"

I dislike the idea of infiltrating someone's mind without their permission. However, stealth might be better for us.

"I can try. Waiting until nightfall could work. If they're asleep, I could pass off my presence as a dream."

"Jesus, you're scary, powerful." Maria chuckles. Her words make me uncomfortable, so I ignore them.

"They're less likely to fight it if they believe it's a dream?" Mohan asks.

"No idea. This is all new to me, too. But it's worth a shot. I don't want to cause harm."

"I think it's smart," Laurance chips in. "If you find nothing, no one is the wiser. If you discover a problem, we still have the element of surprise on our side."

"That's decided then. You'll stay here with us tonight, Erin. I'll call Amelia." Victoria walks away, but I manage to grab her arm gently before she's out of reach.

"She already knows." I smile.

"And what of the Fallen?" Mohan asks. "How do we help them?"

"I'm going to try and call for them. If I can get them together, I can help them before anyone gets hurt."

There is an ache in my belly that has gotten worse since I promised to wait for Amelia before trying to reach out to the escaped vampires. I know I have to keep my word, but I feel sick at the thought of anyone getting hurt. It feels like only a matter of time before chaos erupts.

Is it just a gut feeling? Or something real? God, I wish I could trust myself to know.

Twenty-Two

The atmosphere is significantly lighter. Mohan and Harlan are discussing everything. Victoria is whipping out her culinary skills. And the Loch siblings are being their usual chaotic selves.

Amelia's arrival disperses the last vestiges of anxiety. I'm going to propose a month-long vacation after all this is done. Hawaii couldn't come soon enough.

"Did everything go smoothly?"

Amelia doesn't look stressed in the least, so I presume there were no shouting matches or hearts being broken at Mack's place.

"Everything went fine. Mack was a little surprised to see me."

"Did she ask any questions?"

Chuckling, Amelia draws me into her body. "She looked at me for a while."

"And Jordan?"

"Not a peep. Chris and Mack seem to be getting on well. Jordan joined in the conversation, keeping the longing stares to a minimum."

Leaning up, I kiss her lips. "Did you give me longing looks, Ms. Loch?"

"Mmm."

The hum against my mouth sends frissons of lust to my clit. I can never get enough.

"Oh, I stared longingly. I wanted you so much."

"Hey, before you two start humping in the middle of the dining room, maybe say hello to your family first." Lucille tuts and then walks off.

"Ah, someone's in a better mood." Amelia smiles against my lips.

"Mmm, we talked."

"All sorted?" Her hands have gradually descended to my ass.

"Yes, now you need to stop."

"No fun."

And there's that pout again.

"Later. I'm sure Mohan wants to chat. Eat, catch up with everyone. This will all be over soon, I hope, and then we can get back to the most important thing."

"Us," Amelia replies with one last deep kiss.

Mohan halts his conversation the second he spies Amelia. Rushing to his feet, the much smaller man hugs her fiercely.

"How are you, my dear?"

"I'm okay, Mohan. Thank you for being here. We need you."

Nodding, Mohan picks up his wine glass, clinking it with his pinky ring.

"May I have everyone's attention, please?"

The crowd falls silent, casting their full attention to the Grand Master.

"We are in uncertain times. Our species is growing, and I, for one, am delighted. I have no doubt a higher power sent Erin to us. She alone will save so many suffering souls. I am eternally grateful and offer myself up as your humble servant."

Whoa, what? I know I look like a deer in headlights that are seconds from turning me into roadkill.

"I... Mohan—"

"Erin, my dear, from the second I met you, I knew you were special. We've been looking for a cure for so long, I admit I was at the point of giving up. And even though I wasn't aware of Dr. Mendhi's true activities, I knew he was using Fallen vampires to test out potential cures. Knowing what I know now from the glance you have given me into the suffering of young Chris and Jordan, I'm ashamed of myself for turning a blind eye to what the doctor was doing. I swear to you on the blood of my ancestors, that if I'd known the horrors he was inflicting, I would have stopped him."

Victoria puts a hand on his shoulder. "We know, Mohan."

"That being said, after tonight, we hope to find any parties involved and have them taken into custody immediately. I hope we will also find the Fallen to offer them shelter and aid. Our lives as we know them are changing. Erin's transformation into the Salvator Regina is the dawn of a new time for vampires. As soon as we eliminate the threat, I will confer with the council. Decisions must be made."

"What decisions?" Harlan asks sharing a look with Victoria.

"Decisions regarding our standing in the world."

As much as I want to delve into his meaning, I need everyone to back up a step or two. Mohan is talking about me like I'm some sort of vampire goddess, and it makes me more than uncomfortable. Plus, Amelia is also changing. We seem to be a package deal on the whole savior front.

"Can we all just take a breath," I gasp, unaware how anxious Mohan's speech has made me. "One thing at a time. And please, stop referring to me as Salvator Regina. We don't know what is happening, and until we do, I don't want to chase legends. I'm happy to help the Fallen. Amelia is happy to help their human mates—"

"What do you mean?" Harlan interrupts, looking from me to Amelia. "Amelia?"

"As you know, I've also undergone a few changes."

Mohan is aware now of Amelia's increased speed and strength. I showed him when we connected.

"As much as Erin doesn't wish to follow legends, we have a theory based on the story we've all heard. The queen had a mate. Her mate could turn the human mates of Fallen vampires."

"And you think—"

"I think nothing. As I said, it's a theory. If Erin has similar skills as the legendary queen, it's possible I may have skills like her mate. The moment Erin changed and bit me, I felt my world shift."

Turning away from the many prying eyes, I focus solely on Amelia.

"Did anything happen when you saw Mack?"

"I felt something, but it wasn't strong enough to be conclusive."

"What does it mean if you can change humans?" Aliah calls from across the room.

"Everything and nothing. I'm still me, as Erin is still Erin. We will be able to offer help to vampires who have mated with humans after becoming Fallen."

"This is huge," Mohan erupts, his face full of wonder.

"*This*," Amelia gesticulates, her hands waving from herself to me, "is still a question mark. We deserve the right to figure it out in our own time, without added pressure."

"Of course, of course. But, know that I am here," Mohan answers quickly. "Anything you need."

I swear he looks like he's fighting the urge to bow.

"Food," Victoria shrieks, causing several people, including me, to jump. "We need food, wine, and music. The tension is giving me a headache."

∞

Victoria is a phenomenal cook, or the people she hires are. Either way, I feel almost...normal? No, that's the wrong word. I feel like myself, at least for a little while. I know I have a long night ahead of me, but just for a couple of hours, it's like nothing has changed. I'm just here with my mate and our family, laughing and joking.

I keep a deliberate—metaphorical—ear out for Jordan and Chris, but nothing has come through yet. Hopefully, they're all getting along. Mohan is in the habit of looking at me every few seconds. His eyes dance with expectation. What his expectations are, I'm not sure of.

It's close to one a.m. now, and I'm feeling antsy. I'd like to get my night walk over and done with. Oh, that would make a cool nickname. The nightwalker! Amelia titters next to me as she listens in.

"I think I'm ready to do this," I say to the table.

Harlan stands. "Take my study."

The group grows quiet as I stand and leave. Talk about pressure. Amelia is by my side, her hand hovering over my lower back.

"There is *no* pressure, Erin. None."

"If you say so," I quip, because who are we kidding? There is a ton of pressure to find out if either Noah or Sabine are the assholes helping Dr. Mendhi. If I can't find the answers, who will?

I lay down on Harlan's leather two-seater. Amelia rests a cushion under my head.

"Okay, I'm going in."

Leaning down, Amelia kisses my forehead. "I'll be right here, my love."

Summoning the pictures of Sabine and Noah, I concentrate hard. I find Sabine's light first. Maybe because I've met her and conversed. I've only ever seen Noah in passing. Her mind is fuzzy, and I guess she's taken something to sleep. The drugs are messing with the clarity, but I can still snoop around.

Now that I've done this a couple of times, I find it easier to manipulate the mind to give me access. What I find is upsetting. It's enough to convince me Sabine is in trouble. Delicately extracting myself, careful not to leave a trace of my visit, I search for Noah. His light takes me longer to locate.

Connecting with him isn't as easy either. It's like he has a protective layer around his mind. Eventually I break through, and I immediately know I've found something dark. His mind swirls with dark thoughts, even in sleep.

Suddenly I see piercing black eyes, boring into my mind. He knows I'm there. The urge to run is overwhelming. Taking back control, I force my mind to let go. I sit up, gasping for air.

"Erin?"

I can feel Amelia's hands on my face. My vision is clouded. A shadow lingers, refusing to let me go.

"Amelia?" My voice is sharp and high-pitched, laced with fear. A warmth seeps through the shadow. Amelia's voice echoes around my confused mind.

"I'm here, Erin. Follow my voice."

Her soothing tones gently lead me to safety. The shadow recedes, leaving me feeling nauseous.

"I'm going to be sick."

Air whooshes by as Amelia takes me to the closest bathroom in record time. Her new speed is mighty handy. Once my dinner is in the toilet bowl, I shake. A cold compress settles over my fevered head.

"Let's get you to bed," Amelia murmurs.

"No!" I frantically try to stand. "No, take me to Mohan. Please!"

In powerful arms, I'm taken to Mohan. The whole family watches with concern. I must look crazed.

"Mohan, Erin asked for you."

"Erin, my dear. What happened?"

"Noah, it's him. He's... Oh god, he knows I was there. I don't know how, but he almost trapped me in his mind. Mohan, he knows we're onto the doctor."

"I'll dispatch the guard at once. What of Sabine?"

"She's being blackmailed by Noah."

"I'll have her picked up, too." Mohan pecks me on the temple before standing, his phone already in hand.

My body has stopped shaking. "Red," I mumble.

My hand is guided to a flask. The blood replenishes me instantly, but the fear still lingers. How did Noah do that? How did he know?

Amelia pulls me into her body tighter. Unprepared to let me go. "You need rest, my love."

"We haven't got time. I need to find the Fallen, Amelia."

I can tell she desperately wants to fight me on it, but my hard and unwavering stare finally wins out.

"Fine," she grits out through clenched teeth. "And then you rest."

I nod. "I promise."

As I close my eyes again, preparing myself for yet another journey into the unknown, I take stock of my body. My energy levels are low, and my mind is shaken.

You have to do this now, Erin.

Pushing through, I cast my search out wide. Concentrating on any lights that have a dimmed heart. It's like searching for a needle in a haystack, but what choice do I have?

In the distance, I hear Amelia call for a wet cloth. Am I sweating again? A cool sensation helps me refocus. And there, in the far reaches of my mind, I see specks of light. Willing myself to look harder, I mentally call to them, hoping they are the Fallen that I'm looking for.

Ten beautifully dimmed lights surround me. I can feel their relief as if I were experiencing it myself. My plan isn't to connect, but to send a simple message. *Insomnia, this time tomorrow.*

We hadn't come up with a meeting point, which in hindsight was foolish. Insomnia will be closed by one a.m. We can sneak the Fallen in through the back. Jordan and Chris should be there too, but I simply cannot do anymore. Once the message is sent, my mind revolts, kicking me back to a conscious state, where Amelia's eyes search my face.

"It's done." I sigh.

Twenty-Three

I pass out for nearly fifteen hours before Amelia wakes me up. We need to collect Jordan and Chris and get them over to the penthouse. I thought they'd be with Mack longer than a few hours, but, hey, things need to move fast now.

Mohan assures me he'd have security sent over to the club. Victoria and Harlan organize another fleet of cars to pick us all up. The Lochs plan to meet us at the club later. They're being closed lipped about their destination, up until they meet us. My suspicion is they're meeting with the so-called "resistance" who have been campaigning for vampires to reveal themselves.

The past few weeks are steadily catching up to me. Even though I slept, I still feel exhausted. I just need to push through. Amelia drives us up the coast before heading to Mack's. The salty air and setting sun are a welcome distraction. If I close my eyes, I can imagine us being on vacation, not a care in the world.

"Do you want to stop for five?" Amelia is already pulling over.

Stretching our legs couldn't hurt. Maybe soaking up the last of the sun's rays will give me the boost we need.

"It's just so beautiful here." I sigh into Amelia's embrace. She's holding me from behind as we both stare out into the vast blue stillness.

"It'll be done soon, my love."

"Will it?"

I've been thinking about it. Even if tonight goes smoothly, and I can save the Fallen, even if Noah and Dr. Mendhi are taken into custody. It's not the end. There will always be more Fallen. Then there's the whole coming-out-to-humans thing that needs to be discussed. If that happens, then none of us are going to get any peace for a while. This doesn't feel anywhere near over.

"This part will be done soon. As for the rest, as long as we are together, we can face anything."

"I want us to face a wedding and then living in peaceful bliss."

"And we will. I know it. But, honey, times are changing, and maybe it's time it happened."

I turn in her arms. "You want to come out?"

For as long as I've known Amelia, she has been staunchly against vampires revealing themselves. Although she fell in love and bonded with a human, her distrust of my...their kind is strong.

"You, me, what we're becoming changes things. If there is no reason for humans to distrust us, we may be in with a shot of living in the world."

"God, I hope so. It depends on what Mohan and the council agree on, though."

"True. Who knows what political nonsense will get in the way? But that's not for us to worry about. Right now, we have to focus on the next few hours."

"Then, as much as I'd love to stay here with you, I suppose we should go to Mack's."

Amelia inhales my scent and kisses my neck. "I love you, Ms. Hanson."

"Mmm, I love you, Ms. Loch."

"Let's go."

Sinking into the comfort of the car seat, I let my eyes wander over the scenery, detaching from reality, just for a little while.

Arriving at Mack's, I'm surprised to see Chris sitting on the front porch. The sun has disappeared, and the stars are shining. Another advantage of living outside the city. Less air pollution.

"Hey, whaddya doin' out here, Chris?"

He takes a large gulp of the beer in his hand. "Stick your head in the door, and you'll find out."

Perplexed by his answer, I, of course, open Mack's door and take a step in. One step is all it takes because I'm hit with a wall of moans, sighs, and pants.

Oh, holy hell.

Retreating, I slam the door shut and turn to Chris, who is laughing.

"That's why I'm outside, trying to numb myself with beer."

I go to reply, but I'm interrupted by a scream that rattles the windows.

Wow!

"Well, maybe they're finally finished," Chris mumbles.

"One of them just finished, at least." I laugh. But my smile drops when I see Amelia drop on all fours. Her body is shaking. Suddenly, her head snaps up. Gone are her deep, dark eyes. Fire-red orbs look back at me. I see her fangs fully extended. What looks like blue ink begins to form droplets at the tips.

"Erin," she gasps.

My legs are moving before I can think. Dropping to the ground, I take her by the shoulders. "Amelia, baby, what's happening?"

"I...I need to—" Amelia lets out an unnatural growl that freezes me to the spot. Chris is behind Amelia in a second, his gangly arms wrapping her up in a bear hug.

"Get Jordan and Mack out of here!" he screams. Amelia struggles in his grasp, clawing at his arms. Tears spring in my eyes, my breath catches. Amelia is out of control. "Go! Now!"

Scrambling to my feet, I crash through the front door and run up the stairs.

"Mack?" I scream. Giggling is coming from the bedroom farthest down the hall. This is going to get embarrassing fast. There's no time for knocking or manners. I throw open the door to find Mack wedged between Jordan's legs.

"Erin, what the fuck?"

"Get dressed. We have to go. Now!"

"Erin?" Jordan huffs. "We're a bit busy."

"And you're going to be a bit fucked up if you don't get dressed and get out of this house now! Move!"

I throw discarded clothes at them. Jordan's eyes widen, and I guess she's just gleaned something from my mind.

"Mack, get dressed," she chokes, pulling on clothes.

"Hang the fuck on. What is going on?" Mack's on her knees, naked, hands on hips.

"Honey, please," Jordan pleads.

Mack takes a second to look in Jordan's eyes. Whatever she sees works. Without a hint of protest, Mack dresses. I herd them out of the room and down the stairs. I can still hear Amelia growling and cursing, but she sounds farther away. I hold up my hand to stop them. Sticking my head out the door, I see Chris wrestling Amelia across the yard.

"Get in the car," I shout. Mack and Jordan do as I say, but they both falter in their steps as they see Amelia and Chris.

Slamming my foot on the gas, the car wheel spins. Our escape is met with a wail from behind us. Looking in my mirror, I watch Amelia slump to the floor.

∞

I feel a hand on my arm.

"Erin, stop the car." Jordan firmly grips me. "You're shaking. Stop the car."

What happened? Oh god, Amelia. "I..."

"It's okay, just pull over."

My breath is coming out in shuttered gasps. I do as Jordan asks because I'm not sure I can keep it together much longer.

"What the fuck was that?" Mack all but shrieks in my ear.

"Mack, calm down. You can see what state she's in."

Mack scrubs her face with both hands. "Okay, yeah, okay, sorry, Erin. But, um, could someone explain what that was? I mean, I know it was Amelia, but also, not."

"She... I..."

What had happened? My brain can't compute.

"She changed," Jordan states.

I nod stupidly. "Yes. One minute she was fine, the next..."

"Can you think of anything that happened in the moments before?"

"Well, one of you screamed like a fucking banshee," I shoot back. "Maybe she thought we were under attack."

I see in the rearview, Mack has gone bright red. "We, um..."

"We bonded, Erin," Jordan beams.

I would be thrilled for them if my mate hadn't just turned feral. A thought flickers like an ember, gradually catching fire.

"You bonded?" Turning in my seat, I look from Jordan to Mack. "When you...you know, for the last time before I came barging in, that's when you bonded?"

"Yes," Mack says. "I've never felt anything like it." She's leaning over, nuzzling Jordan.

"It was magical," Jordan replies.

"You know what this means?" I ask.

Mack sits up. Her eyes are firmly on Jordan. "I understand. Jordan explained everything."

"You know it's more complicated with Jordan already past her thirtieth birthday?"

A current of hope fizzles through my chest.

"Yes. But, it doesn't matter. We're meant to be together, for however long that's possible."

"Maybe, or maybe that's why Amelia changed."

Of course it is. It's too much of a coincidence to be anything else. Amelia already believes she may have the power to change a Fallen's human mate.

Everything is slotting into place. Just like my thirst overwhelmed me the first time, so has Amelia's. Mack is the first human she's come across who has bonded with her mate. I'm only guessing, but I believe the second that bond cemented, Amelia turned. Her—now—natural instinct is to change Mack so she can be with Jordan for eternity.

Jordan takes a second to poke at my mind. For once, I happily let her in. "You think…"

"I do. But you two need to have a conversation. And I'm sorry, but it can't wait."

I slip out of the car, leaving a stunned Jordan and confused Mack to talk. This is a huge decision for both of them. If Mack chooses not to change, I'm going to have to take Amelia far away for a while until she gets the urge to nibble on my ex out of her system.

The night is bitter, but my relentless pacing around the car keeps me from getting hypothermia. I've no idea how much time has passed. My thoughts are far too chaotic to take notice of such a thing.

The car door opening grinds me to a halt. Literally, I walk into the fucking thing and almost end up on my ass.

"Sorry." Jordan grins.

"How did it go?" I turn to look as Mack climbs out behind Jordan.

"Amelia can try to change me. If you think that's what she's made to do."

"Mack, are you sure? This is a huge decision."

"I know." Mack nods. She pulls Jordan to her side, kissing her temple. "Under normal," she barks out a laugh, "sorry, *usual* circumstances, I know we would have had more time to think about our future. But, honestly, Erin, I can't even stomach the idea of Jordan having to live without me if I remain human. I turned thirty a few weeks ago. I'm ready."

"Have you thought about your family?"

"We tried to talk about all aspects of it. And we're confident we can get through it. I only have my dad, who's usually balls deep in a bottle every night. I can change jobs if necessary."

Is it weird I'm slightly envious they came to the decision much faster than Amelia and me? We danced around for months.

"So, do you want to go back?"

With one more shared look, they nod.

"Okay, let's go. We still have a bunch of Fallen to save before the night is over."

Lord, I hope I'm right about Amelia. Jordan and Chris are fast and strong though, so I trust them to keep Mack safe, if I'm wrong.

We're all silent as we approach Mack's house again. There are lights on in the lower rooms. I connect to Amelia and know she is calmer, but the closer we get, the more agitated she becomes.

Mack steps out of the car, her face pale. Jordan is by her side, holding her hand. Looking at the front door, we hear Amelia racing through the house. And then she's there. Blood-red eyes and fangs. Her gaze solely on Mack.

"Mack," Amelia begins, her voice hoarse. "You have mated with a Fallen?"

Mack draws in a deep breath, squaring her shoulders. "Yes."

"I can hear your soul," Amelia continues. "Torn between elation and despair. You have found your missing piece, but you cannot live with her for eternity in your human form."

Amelia hasn't even glanced my way. I don't think she's even aware anyone else is here. I open my mouth to speak, but Chris subtly shakes his head.

"If you so wish, I can give you immortality, Mack." Amelia takes a steady step forward.

"Bite me," Mack replies, and if I didn't think she actually meant it, I'd laugh my ass off.

Twenty-Four

Chris, Jordan, and I hold our collective breaths as Mack takes a step toward Amelia.

"I said bite me," Mack repeats, cocking her head to the side, revealing more of her neck.

"I heard you the first time." Amelia has composed herself. I can see it in her eyes how badly she wants to drink from Mack, but she's not allowing that drive to overtake her senses. Not this time, at least. "One last time. You understand what this means?"

"Yes. I do, and I consent. Do whatever you have to do, Amelia. Please."

With an almost unperceivable nod, Amelia closes the distance between them. She looks formidable in her current state, but Mack isn't frightened.

"Hold still."

We watch Amelia slowly lower herself. Her fangs are dripping, and I see the way she's tensing her jaw muscles, determined to stay in control. My fingers twitch, because all I want to do is reach out to my mate.

The atmosphere is charged as we watch in slow motion. Amelia's fangs slice through Mack's skin easily. Blood oozes out of the wounds, but Amelia quickly laps it up. Seconds go by. Is Amelia having trouble stopping? I remember what that felt like and my heart rate picks up. Jordan takes a cautionary step forward, but it's unnecessary as Amelia pulls back, pushing herself from Mack.

Turning on her heels, Amelia spits out Mack's blood. She's clutching her stomach, gagging. Mack falls to her knees, supported by Jordan.

"Baby," I call, rushing to Amelia's side. "Talk to me."

After several more rounds of gagging, she finally turns to me. "Mack tastes like shit."

Laughter rings out of me involuntarily.

"How is she?"

Jordan cups Mack's face, looking into her eyes. Eyes that share a striking similarity with Jordan and Chris's.

"Okay, she seems okay. And you?"

"Better. The thirst has gone."

I brush Amelia's forehead. "Do you...do you crave human blood now?"

"Good Lord, no!" Amelia shakes her head. "My stomach is still in revolt from the little I just had."

"But? That doesn't make sense."

"All because my job is to help turn humans, doesn't mean I want to drink from them, Erin. I can't think of anything worse."

"So you're telling me you're going to vomit every time?"

"Yes, but it's worth it. Look."

We turn back to Jordan and Mack, who are kissing sweetly.

"So, that was intense." Chris laughs, breaking the moment. I shoot him a mock scowl. "What?"

"Way to ruin it, Chris."

"I had to listen to them humping. I'd say it's my right."

Jordan and Mack turn red but chuckle along.

Confident Amelia is okay, I go to Mack, who is still on her knees. My eyes shift to her neck. The puncture wounds close quickly and disappear. "Mack, how are you?"

"Good, I feel good."

"Immortal?" Jordan asks, eyebrow raised.

"Possibly. How is it *supposed* to feel?"

Scoffing playfully, I hold my hand up. "Don't ask me. I haven't done anything by the book so far."

"There isn't a defining feeling. You just know," Amelia replies, she's slowly righting herself. I'm happy to see her beautiful eyes are back and her fangs have gone.

"Then, yes, I believe I am immortal."

"After all this is done, and we're married, I'm throwing one hell of a party." I laugh.

"We still have things to do, my love." Amelia takes a deep breath. "We must get to the club."

"Are you strong enough, or do you want to stay home?" Jordan asks Mack.

"If you're going, then so am I."

"All right, let's get on our way."

Mack and Jordan take a separate car. Chris rides with me and Amelia.

"You're one strong lady," Chris says, breaking the silence ten minutes into the journey.

"Sorry. I wasn't in my right mind. I didn't hurt you, did I?" Amelia looks at Chris in her rearview. Her eyes hold concern.

"Nah, I might be skinny, but I'm no pushover. You feeling better?"

"Much. Although I need to get a handle on this new side of myself. I can't react that way the next time a human bonds."

"I don't think you will," I chime in. "I was frenzied like that when I bit you. It was different when Jordan fed from me, too. By the time I got to Chris, that hurried, unstoppable thirst had transformed into something I could control. Now your first is out of the way. I'd bet the next time will be easier." Laying my hand on her thigh, I squeeze gently.

"I hope so. I know how I must've looked to you all."

"Like one scary motherfucker." Chris laughs, earning another scowl from me.

"Don't give him that look, love. He's right."

"Still, a little more tact wouldn't go amiss, Chris."

"My bad. But look, it's done now. Mack is immortal, we think, and happily in love with Jordan. However, I request a change of venue. If I have to continue hiding out. I can't be subject to the noises that pair are going to make

272

when they get home. It's unnerving, and I'll be scarred for life."

Amelia cracks a smile. "I think you've earned the right to a peaceful place to stay. We'll find you a bed, don't worry."

"Hopefully it won't be necessary," I add. "After tonight, it should be over, right?"

"I hope so, my love."

Shoving his head between the seats, Chris turns serious. "What's the plan?"

"If the Fallen received my message, they will be at Insomnia around two. Mohan is sending extra security, just to be on the safe side."

"Did you weed out the traitors?" Chris hisses his question.

"Yes, but there was a hiccup. Noah, Mohan's second in command, knew I was in his mind. He knows the council is coming for him. That's why the Grand Master wants extra bodies."

"You think Noah will try to get to the Fallen at the club? That's brazen, don't you think?"

"Is it? Noah is burned. There's no point in hiding. He'll want to get rid of the evidence, though."

"By killing the vampires he helped torture?"

"Yes," I breathe, noting Chris's eyes well up with tears.

"And the doctor?" Amelia asks. "Did Mohan give you any idea what he plans to do with Mendhi?"

"No, and I didn't ask. My focus was getting the Fallen somewhere safe. I'm sure Mohan has everything under control."

We arrive at Insomnia and notice the unusually high number of cars lining the back street. The club is open as usual, with happy patrons dancing and drinking without a care in the world.

Heading directly for the hidden stairs, I see several men and women who are definitely with Mohan's security team. Amelia notices them too, giving a quick nod of acknowledgment.

Upstairs, the penthouse is full to the brim. Council members, other security personnel, and the Lochs are mingling, discussing the possible outcomes of tonight.

"There you are," Victoria calls from the other side of the room. "We thought you'd be here well before now."

"Something came up," Amelia answers, leaving no room for further discussion. "This is a lot of people."

"Well, of course. Noah's in the wind—"

"What?"

A deafening silence descends on the room as I speak.

"What do you mean?"

Harlan steps forward. "When Mohan sent his team to pick up Noah, he was gone. Left in a hurry."

"Damn," Amelia growls. "So now what?"

"We proceed as planned. The Fallen need your help, Erin."

"And what if Noah turns up?"

"We have half a vampire army standing by. We'll protect them and you." Harlan puts his arm around Victoria.

"I'll protect you," Amelia whispers with conviction.

"Okay," I begin. It's time I got a grip. "We still have a few hours. Everyone, make sure you have enough Red and rest. I'm going to lie down for a while."

Amelia follows closely behind. We need some time together, away from the chaos and uncertainty. Stripping off my clothes, I head straight to bed. The sheets are cool and comforting. Amelia slips in behind me, pulling me into her. Soft, warm breath tickles my neck. If I didn't think

I needed some sleep, I'd be taking advantage of our alone time. However, I have a feeling things are going to get nuts later on and I'm going to need my strength.

Light tapping on my shoulder wakes me up. Amelia is sitting on the bed, her face soft from sleep. "It's time to get up, my love."

I nod because I haven't got the words right now. We shower and dress silently. The vibe in the room is markedly different from when we arrived earlier. The Loch clan is chattering among themselves quietly. The council members are sitting with their eyes closed. I wonder if they're meditating or something. As for the other security people, I presume they've already gone downstairs.

Insomnia is now officially closed. Claire and Kit will head home within the next twenty minutes. I'm sure they will both be pissed when they find out we kept this from them, but it's for their safety.

The penthouse is feeling claustrophobic with so many people still here. I need to go downstairs and...prepare? I'm not sure if there is anything to do but wait. We have half an hour until two a.m.

Amelia reads my thoughts and escorts me downstairs. The club is empty except for the security, Kit and Claire.

Claire glares at us, obviously aware something is happening. Amelia strokes the base of my spine lovingly.

"I'll be right back."

I'm more than happy to let Amelia deal with Claire and Kit. I need to focus. Actually, I need a drink. Slamming a shot of rum helps. I stop myself from having a second. With no idea what alcohol does to my abilities, I need to be sensible. But, damn, does the bottle look tempting!

Finding a quiet corner, I sit, closing my eyes and quieting my mind. I listen, hoping to hear or see something that tells me the vampires are okay. Their lights are distant but present, which helps soothe me.

A shift in the air causes me to open my eyes and focus on the room. Then security people are lining the walls, talking into their concealed microphones. It's almost two. Amelia is talking to her parents, who have settled in a booth not too far from me. Everyone is here and waiting.

I feel them before I see them. Their desperation and pain echoes through me like a siren's call. I'm drawn to them. I stand and make my way to the bar. My body facing the back entrance. With shaking hands, I steady myself. I can also feel Amelia's protectiveness surround me, trying to calm my nerves.

One by one Fallen vampires enter the club, looking terrified, hopeful, and wary all in the same breath. Their eyes find me instantly and I can see their relief.

"Welcome," I say calmly. "You're safe now."

I'm stuck in place when they drop to their knees, bowing their heads.

Wow, okay.

"Please," one vampire stutters. Her eyes are red, her face is scarred, and she looks like she hasn't had a decent meal in weeks. "Everything hurts," she cries.

"Help them up," I say to the room. "Get them seated comfortably." The Loch family are the first to respond. "I'll start now, but in the meantime, give them Red."

Heading to the woman who spoke, I kneel in front of her. My fangs reveal themselves easily. They've become an extension of me, literally I know, but it's more than that. I feel them drip with serum. The young girl pushes her hair off her shoulder with shaking limbs. Her eyes plead with me to stop the pain. I've waited long enough.

My fangs pierce her skin and I feel her blood coat my tongue. As with Chris, it tastes tainted. My venom mixes easily, so I pull back. I know I won't take too much from her. It's as easy as breathing now. My limits are clear.

The woman slouches. Lucas appears behind her to support her weight.

"Get her laid down."

Lucas nods and sets to work.

Twenty-Five

"How many is that?" Amelia brushes a strand of hair from my face.

"Seventeen."

"You need a break, Erin."

She's not wrong. I'd prepared for ten Fallen, but I was looking at closer to thirty.

"Let me help three more and then I'll rest for half an hour, okay?"

I know she's unhappy, but me getting a little rest pales in comparison to what these vampires need. They've waited long enough.

"We're taking the cured vampires up to the penthouse. Mohan sent another doctor to check them over."

"And once they get the all-clear?"

"We haven't got that far yet." She sighs.

"Maybe we can help," Victoria asks. "Between us all, the family has more than enough spare rooms to accommodate."

"And if more show up?" Which they will. We have been grievously misled about the number of Fallen in LA alone. I shudder to think how many are in the world, suffering.

Harlan plants a hand on my forearm. "Then we figure it out."

"You look tired, my dear." Victoria looks at me with such compassion, I have the urge to cry. Maybe it's the residual feelings from the Fallen still pinballing around my body.

"Three more. Then, I'll rest."

The back door rattles open as seven more Fallen make their way toward the crowd.

My heart drops. "I..."

"Mother, Father, we need to change the plan. Erin simply can't get through them all tonight."

"Agreed. Let's organize to have everyone taken back to the house."

"I'm still going to have to do it, eventually," I protest. "Might as well be now."

Amelia shakes her head. "You're pale, and I can hear how tired your mind is. I know they need help, my love, but you are one person."

"Wait, you said there is a doctor here?" Why didn't I think of it sooner? "Call her. I need to ask her something."

Amelia forgoes calling and leaves immediately. Seconds later, she reappears, practically carrying a very surprised doctor in her arms.

"Here, this is Dr. Chord."

"That was some ride." The doctor laughs. "Erin, how can I help?"

She's a short woman and looks to be maybe in her mid-forties in human years. God knows how old she really is.

"Ninety," Amelia blurts out. "She's ninety."

"Ah, I see the mind-reading thing is true then." Dr. Chord chuckles, her whole demeanor relaxed, which I find comforting. Right, back to the topic at hand.

"Dr. Chord—"

"Riley, call me Riley."

"Riley, do you think you could extract the serum from my fangs?"

"It's possible."

"We need a way to fast track this," I say, waving my hands around the room. "I can't bite them all tonight. It's draining me."

"Ah, and you think I could extract the serum and inject them that way?"

I nod. "Do you think it would work?"

"I can't see why not. Shall we try?"

It's going to be a cakewalk getting the serum. My fangs have been on overdrive since the Fallen arrived. Taking out surgical gloves and several empty vials, Riley pulls up a stool and sits in front of me.

"Open up then." She smiles.

I widen my mouth. I can feel the serum dripping. Closing my eyes, I think of all the vampires still in pain.

"Wow, you're producing a lot," Lucille comments. I didn't even see her standing there.

"Okay Erin, that should do for now."

Opening my eyes, I stare at three vials of gold liquid.

"Is that it?"

Ridiculous question because of course that's it. I look at Amelia, who understands. Her venom or serum, however you want to describe it, is blue. And mine gold. Just like the lights we saw when we bonded and have seen every time since. What does it mean?

"I'll need a volunteer," the doctor continues.

"Me!" a man says. He's limping, holding his arm close to his chest. "Please, let me."

Dr. Chord fills a small syringe. "Okay, keep still."

The man stands still, looking into my eyes as the doctor injects half the syringe's content into his arm. I smile at him, hoping it brings him some comfort. We watch as his eyes turn golden. It worked. He begins to cry, and I join him.

"Oh, thank god." My voice is choked on unshed tears. "Doctor, take what you need." I ready myself for another extraction.

"Everyone, be ready to help," Victoria calls.

As soon as the doctor has enough syringes and serum, we can finally help them all.

Some vampires help the Fallen into comfy chairs, rolling up their sleeves. Others hand out flasks of Red. Amelia stands by my side as Riley takes more serum. Everyone is working flawlessly together. An hour later, all the Fallen have been given a shot.

"And we're done," Riley exclaims with a bright smile. Amazing anyone can look that pleased at four in the morning.

"Mother and Father have two minibus vans waiting by the back entrance. We need to get all the Fall—sorry, cured vampires in them," Marcus says.

"This is the last bit, babe," Amelia coos. She doesn't often call me babe, only when she's tired.

"Okay, last push. Let's do this."

Once again, we come together as a unit, seamlessly working together to get the newly cured vampires into the vans. Harlan and Victoria head out first, trailed by the rest of the Loch clan.

As soon as the last minivan pulls away, I collapse into the nearest chair.

"My god, I could sleep for a week."

"Mmmm," Amelia sleepily replies. "Do you want to stay here tonight?"

"Yes, I can't face a car journey at this hour."

"I'll get cleaned up and meet you upstairs in a few minutes."

"Baby, the cleanup can wait."

"It's not fair to leave it to anyone else. We need to be at my parents' first thing tomorrow, and we have no idea when we'll get a chance to come back. Claire will tear my brand-new fangs out and wear them as a necklace if she walks into this."

I manage a soft chuckle. "Yeah, she'll have both our asses."

The club is littered with glasses, empty flasks, and discarded needles.

"I'll stay and help, the—"

Towering over me, Amelia gives me her best intimidating glare. "Nope, bed, now."

"You know you get me hot when you get bossy." I smile.

Rolling her eyes, Amelia turns me by my shoulders, marching me to the stairs.

"You're unbelievable sometimes, Ms. Hanson."

"Why thank you, Ms. Loch. Don't be too long."

We kiss for several seconds, luxuriating in our aloneness.

"Go," she finally whispers against my lips.

I liken the stairs up to the penthouse to a twelve-hour hike. That's how long it feels to have finally reached home. The lights are off, but that's fine. I just want to crash. Amelia will carry me to bed if I collapse on the sofa.

"I wondered how long I'd have to wait." The voice in the darkness whispers.

Trying to remain calm, I stroll over to the kitchen counter and begin pouring myself a drink. I want to scream and shout, but there's no point. I try in vain to call for Amelia, but I'm blocked from the outside world.

"Drink?" My voice remains steady, but my insides are putty.

The lamp by the armchair Noah is sitting in illuminates the room. "No, thank you. I won't be staying long enough."

"What can I help you with, Noah?"

"Nothing," he simply states.

"Then why are you in my home?"

"I wanted to get a look at the so-called Salvator Regina. You've amassed quite the following, haven't you, Erin?"

My name on his tongue burns my ears.

"I also wanted to meet the person who invaded my mind. I've never met anyone else who is capable. Not even the oh-so-mighty Grand Master."

"Well, ta-da. Here I am. You've met me. Now you can go, before god knows how many security people come bursting in here to take you away."

Scoffing, Noah leans forward. "Ah yes. You all want to see me locked away for my terrible crimes."

"You tortured them," I gasp. "Some for decades."

"So what!" Noah exclaims. "No one gave them a second thought. Even good old Mohan let them get experimented on."

"He thought Dr. Mendhi was testing out cures!"

"That may be so, but he didn't look too close, did he? Hmm?"

"He trusted Mendhi. He trusted you!"

"And that's his mistake. The Fallen are our lab rats. Have been for decades. It's the way we work. All because Mohan didn't sign off, doesn't mean he did anything to stop it either. You all want me and the doctor to be the bad guys. Fine. I'll do what needs to be done to secure our survival."

"Do you hear yourself? Vampires are surviving. There is no threat."

"You're right, I misspoke. I'm the one that will take us from the shadows and into the light. I will lead our species to where they belong. At the top of the food chain."

"All of this because you want...what, to best the humans?"

Noah rises from the chair. I swallow hard because, Jesus Christ, he's big.

"We are better than humans. Period. Mohan would have us continue to skulk around, hiding. Well, no more."

"What's that got to do with the Fallen and the horrific things you've been doing to them?"

"Insurance, dear Erin."

"I don't understand?"

As we speak, I try to edge subtly toward the door.

"I wouldn't move any closer to the door if I were you. Not unless you want Amelia to suffer the consequences."

My heart freezes. Oh god, does he have Amelia? I shouldn't have left her. Stopping, I take several breaths. "Okay, what's next?"

He hasn't come here for small talk.

"Next. You die. Erin, you've done a valiant job curing those lost souls. However, I have to insist you stop. Now we both know if I leave you alive, you won't be able to help yourself. So, logic dictates I take you off the board. I still need test subjects, and that's proving rather difficult with you trying to turn them all. So, you die. Problem solved."

I watch him reach around his back, pulling something from his belt.

"You don't have to do this," I try. My voice is on the edge of pleading.

"I don't have to, I suppose." He cocks the gun. "But I want to?"

I'd love to say my life flashes in front of my face. It doesn't. I'm only consumed with fear. Fear of what the loss will do to Amelia. I've never had a problem with dying. It's a part of life, isn't it? But Amelia? My god, this will kill her too.

"I swear to you, Noah, Amelia will rip you limb from limb."

"I'm sure she'll try."

I summon every last particle of strength and try to break through whatever shield he has trapping my mind.

Help me.

Everything happens in a split second. My world slows down to a crawl. Everything's in slow motion, as I see Noah squeeze the trigger. Amelia's bone-shattering scream rocks the building, but it's too late. I feel the impact.

Unlike the movies, I'm not thrown back dramatically. Dropping to my knees, I look down at my chest, watching as the crimson stain grows bigger through my top. The air is stolen from my lungs.

Stunned, I look back up at Noah. He tucks the gun away and vanishes through the sliding doors. Moments later, Amelia crashes through the door, sending it flying across the room.

"Erin!" she screams.

"A-Amelia," I choke. Blood spills from my mouth. "I'm sorry, baby," I sputter.

I'm so sorry for what she is about to witness, and for every morsel of pain she's going to feel once I'm gone.

"Erin, love, hold on. Just stay with me." She fumbles with her phone, her entire body shaking.

I bask in my last few minutes on this Earth, tucked into her chest. There is no place I would rather be when I take my last breath.

Twenty-Six

O uch, Jesus, mother of—

"She's not dead!" The sound of Amelia's voice reverberates around my pounding head.

"Amelia, darling, she's gone. You need to let her go."

A footstep grows closer.

"Take one more step and I'll rip all of you to shreds. Do you hear me? You are not taking her!"

Another step. This one is heavier, though.

"Victoria, let her be."

"Harlan, we need to move Erin's body."

Amelia clutches me tighter as her mother speaks.

"She. Is. Not. Dead!"

I feel Amelia's anger vibrating through the air.

Okay, so everything hurts and my head feels like it's stuffed with cotton balls. Pain is radiating from my chest. Checking in with my body, I notice my limbs feel heavy, and I can't move them. That might be because I'm still unconscious, though. My hearing seems good. Hopefully, the rest of my bodily functions will catch up soon.

Amelia's body holds me even tighter, which, as wonderful as that is, isn't helping my breathing situation. Can't she feel me? I can smell her perfume, I can feel her hair brushing over my face...and tears. I can feel her tears on my face. How long have I been down?

Shuffling sounds interrupt the sound of Amelia crying.

"Amelia?"

"Lucille, she's not dead! I'd know it. My soul would feel torn in two if Erin were dead. She's gone, but she's not dead."

"What do you mean she's gone, honey?" Harlan asks tentatively.

"I can't find her thoughts. Our link is gone."

I'm jostled slightly as Amelia lays my body down carefully. I feel her lips on mine, and then they're gone.

"You're not taking her anywhere, Mother." Her tone is dangerous.

"Amelia, my sweet child." Victoria's voice cracks. "I know this is impossible, but we can't keep her here."

Slowly, I feel my muscles respond to the commands I'm yelling at them in my head. Amelia is getting more agitated, and I can sense that the "new" side of her personality is about to make an appearance. The low growl I hear traveling up her throat leads me to scream louder in my head. Amelia will regret going full scary vampire on her family. They've yet to see her fully unleashed.

"Mmother—" I mumble, willing my mouth and voice box to work. They must have heard something, because Amelia is by my side in an instant, cradling my face. I hear other footsteps move closer, too.

"Erin? Erin, my love?"

"Mmmother. Fffucker."

Now my cognitive function is back up and running, my brain processes how much I hurt. Getting slugged in the chest is no fun at all!

Amelia bursts out laughing, which quickly turns to sobbing. Her face is buried in my neck.

"Shit, she's alive," I hear Aliah choke.

"Erin, open your eyes."

Oh right, they're still closed. Prying them open, my vision swims and I feel a wave of nausea roll through my stomach.

"Gently try to sit her up, Amelia." Victoria's voice is closer and softer.

"Come on, honey."

I clench my teeth as Amelia sits me up slightly.

"Are you going to vomit?"

I shake my head slowly. "No. My. Chest. Hurts."

"Mother, can you hold her up?" Victoria slips behind me as Amelia kneels in front of me. I feel her lift my top. My eyes are still fuzzy.

"Nothing," Amelia whispers. "Not a trace."

"How is that possible?" Laurence calls.

"We've been asking that question a lot," I wheeze out.

Victoria leans in. "Can you stand?"

"I think so."

When my butt finally hits the couch, I let out a strangled breath.

"Oh, my chest feels tight."

My lungs feel trapped in a vise.

Amelia lifts my chin with her hand. Her eyes are glassy and red. "I'm not surprised. You took a round to the heart!"

Looking into her eyes, I see the fear and pain still clinging to her very essence. Leaning forward, I take her lips in mine.

"I can feel you again," I whisper. Our connection is back.

"Can you *please* stop leaving me?" She chokes, tears streaming down her face once again.

"Oh, baby."

As much as it hurts to move, I need to hold her, comfort her, and yes, stop fucking leaving her.

We stay locked together for a few minutes until Victoria pulls our attention back.

"Dr. Chord is here."

Weaving her way through the crowd, Riley drops her medical bag next to me and takes a seat.

"Erin, you've been in the wars."

"You could say that." I grin.

"Can I look?"

Leaning back, I gingerly lift my top up and over my head. It's ruined by the bloodstain and massive hole.

Damn, I really liked that top.

Looking down, I see skin that is stained red, but that's it. No gaping hole, not even a scratch.

My fingers roam over the area, looking for some sign I'd taken a bullet to the chest. "How?"

"How indeed," Riley comments, her fingers palpating the area. "Could we have a little privacy?"

It's only then I see the entire Loch family staring at my chest. Thankfully, I put a good bra on today.

Harlan clears his throat. "We'll go downstairs."

"Does this hurt?" Riley presses different parts of my breastbone.

"It feels bruised."

"I'd like to scan your chest. I can't feel anything abnormal, but I want to make sure there is no internal damage."

As Riley unpacks her medical bag, which includes a portable ultrasound machine, Amelia picks up my discarded shirt, shaking it out. The clink of metal hitting the floor turns our heads.

Bending, Amelia picks up the chunk of metal. "It's the bullet."

Riley takes the mangled shard, inspecting it. "It definitely hit you. Look how deformed it is. And it has blood on it."

"If it hit me, how did it end up coming back out?"

297

"How are you a vampire through spontaneous transformation? How are you and Amelia able to communicate the way you do? How can you reach other minds? How can you cure the Fallen?"

"It would be nice if we could answer just one of those," I mutter.

∞

"Everything looks good. No damage whatsoever." Riley studies the images on her portable scanner. We've been at it for hours. She's prodded, poked, and done all other manner of things and yet, Riley still can't find anything amiss.

"So this is another manifestation of Erin's transformation," Amelia comments, her gaze somewhere out over the horizon.

"I'd say so."

"Are you suggesting I am invincible?"

Everyone thinks that being immortal means being unable to die at all. That's wrong. As an immortal, we will not decay. We are undying. But that certainly doesn't mean we can't be killed.

Cocking her head, Riley studies me. "Can I test something out?"

"Sure." What have I got to lose?

Picking up a scalpel, Riley slices my arm several times.

"Fuck! What the hell?" I might not die, but I can feel pain. Holy crap.

Amelia grabs Riley's hand holding the scalpel and squeezes. Riley gasps in pain.

"L-look," she begs. Her eyes are wildly looking between Amelia and my arm.

"Amelia, look."

I can't believe what I'm seeing. They're closing. The wounds are vanishing before my eyes. Amelia finally tears her death stare from Riley. Dropping the doctor's hand, she kneels before me, taking my arm.

"You're healing." Grabbing a tissue, she cleans the area. Again, my skin is stained red, but no trace of the slashes.

"We need Barty. He must have found something more by now."

Even I'm buying into the whole I-am-a-reincarnated-vampire-queen thing.

Standing, Amelia furrows her eyebrows. Turning, she grabs the scalpel, plunging it into her stomach. My world spins and the floor shifts. What has she just done?

Riley rushes forward, pressing the wound with her hand. "Amelia, I need you—"

With a grunt, Amelia retracts the knife, dropping it to the floor. Ripping off her top, she stares down. My eyes travel the length of her body.

"Oh, my god."

Riley wipes the area, her eyes wide. "But...what?"

"We are one, Erin. It makes sense I can heal, too."

I want to wipe that smug look off her face with a smack upside the head.

"And you thought stabbing yourself in front of me was the best way to check it out? Are you insane?"

"My love—"

"Don't you 'my love' me, Amelia Loch! What if you had been wrong? I can't believe you—"

Soft warm lips engulf my mouth. Her tongue dances with my own, rendering me speechless and breathless.

"That's not fair," I gasp, my lips searching for hers once again.

"It's my only weapon against you." She smiles. "You're right to be mad. That was thoughtless."

"Yes, it was."

"But I was right."

Pulling back, I look up into her gorgeous eyes. They're still red from all the crying she did, but they sparkle again now. Her hair hangs down in perfect silky strands. She is magnificent.

"You were right. But I never want to see anything like that again."

"Agreed. That was traumatizing," Riley adds. "Now, let's review, shall we? Both of you seem to be invincible."

We nod.

"And none of us know how or why you have developed that...ability?"

Another nod.

"Okay. Well, my work is done. From a medical point of view, I can't find a damn thing. Your blood is pure vampire now, Erin. I looked over the tests performed by Mendhi when you first began transforming. Apart from the fact it's a miracle a human can change, there was nothing out of the ordinary. I compared your results to Anya's. Identical. I cannot find a reason, within your genome, to explain these advanced—"

"Abilities," I finish.

"Exactly. For once, I'm completely stumped."

"When, may I ask, did you have time to do all these comparisons and tests?" Amelia asks. "You've only been Erin's doctor for a few hours."

"Ah yes, well. Mohan and your mother had me look at Mendhi's results."

"They didn't trust him to tell us the whole truth?"

"I think they just wanted a second opinion. Mendhi didn't mind either. You are a brand-new variant of vampire. He was happy to have an extra pair of eyes."

"Variant?"

"Yes. You two are a one-of-a-kind pair." Riley chuckles at herself.

I shake my head. "Not quite. Noah can manipulate minds as well. He blocked me from calling to Amelia."

"Hmm, okay, that's certainly interesting. Did he display any other abilities, similar to your own?"

"No. I was able to break through the shield eventually." I look at Amelia. "I think."

"I heard you."

Tucking myself into her embrace, I take several gigantic breaths, bathing my olfactory system in her scent.

"I'll relay that back to Mohan. He needs to know before attempting to apprehend Noah."

"I need to talk to Mohan." I can't believe it's taken me so long to think about it. "Noah had plenty to say before...you know."

Giving me a kiss, Amelia breaks away. I miss her instantly. Heading to the table, she picks up her phone. "I'll call Mohan and Barty."

"Where *are* Anya and Barty?"

"Meeting with a friend."

Our lives have been a whirlwind. I can't keep track of everyone.

"Barty thought it best to carry on researching while we dealt with the Fallen."

"I'll head downstairs and let your family know they can come back up. I'm sure they're anxious to see you both."

Jesus, I forgot all about them, too.

"Please. And Riley. Thank you."

"My pleasure. Call if you need anything."

A few seconds pass as we listen to Riley descend.

"Baby, I need to clean up. It's only going to upset everyone if they see all this blood. You should change, too. And maybe don't tell your mother you stabbed yourself."

"You did what?" Victoria's voice reaches the rafters. "Amelia Loch, explain yourself."

Amelia glares at me, causing me to roll my lips. I'm going to do the awkward laugh-at-an-inappropriate-time-thing.

"I'm just gonna..." Turning on my heel, I grab my blood-soaked top and hightail it to the bathroom. Victoria's sonic-level voice remains audible, even when I close the door.

Oops.

Twenty-Seven

"Yes. Right there. Mm hmm. Harder. Oh, yes!"

"My love, you're so wet."

Damn right I'm wet. I've had Amelia working me into a frenzy ever since we banished the family to have a little alone time.

Re-establishing a firm grip on the headboard, I dip my upper body, allowing Amelia even better access.

"Nice and deep, baby." I pant.

"Mmm, how's that?"

That is exquisite. I can feel the toy deep inside. We started on the couch with sweet, tender kisses and soft, loving touches. Amelia gave me two orgasms there before she hiked me over her shoulder and sprinted to the bed. The orgasm rapidly building is number three in the bedroom. First was me straddling her lap as she plunged her fingers inside, nipping at my neck. Second, was sitting on her face, and this third one. Well, it's my favorite position. Amelia driving our favorite toy into me from behind.

Her body responds just as urgently as mine when we make love like this. I can feel her quivering. Her hands hold my hips tightly as she thrusts hard. I know she's about to come when she grabs a handful of my hair. God, I love it.

"I'm so close, Erin," she pants, her thrusts becoming erratic.

"More, a little more," I gasp, knowing it's a matter of seconds before I lose control completely. And then Amelia brings her free hand around to my clit and all bets are off. I can't hold on.

My scream combines with Amelia's deep guttural moan, sending literal gold and blue sparks into the air. I wish I could keep my eyes open long enough to watch them explode around us like fireworks. I collapse, with Amelia following, still buried deep inside me.

"Oh, that was wonderful," I croon. "I've missed you."

"And I you."

"I'm not sure your mother will forgive us anytime soon for kicking them all out."

"Darling, can we please not mention my mother when we're naked?"

Giggling, I roll over. Amelia shifts to the side, allowing my body to seamlessly slot next to hers. The gentle way she strokes my hair sends me into a trance.

"Mmmm, okay, not talking about parents."

A sadness washes over me. My parents still haven't reached out to me.

"They didn't mean it, honey. They love you. When all this craziness is over, go and see them. I promise you they will wrap themselves around you."

"I hope you're right, Amelia. And it's still strange sometimes when you do that!"

"What? Hear your thoughts?"

"Yes."

"Honestly, I've tried to limit doing it. But when you're full of emotion, they come over to me on a loudspeaker."

"I don't mind, baby. It's nice to have you comfort me without me having to utter a word."

"But that doesn't mean we stop speaking. I don't want you lost in your thoughts, waiting for me to hear. Communication, my love, is interaction. I want you to come to me and tell me what you need. Tell me your worries."

"Okay. I'll try harder. Sometimes the thoughts just appear."

"But I won't always be close by or tuned in to hear them. In that case, I'd like you to find me and talk to me. If we ever have kids—"

"Kids? We're not even married yet, Ms. Loch."

"I said when." Amelia chuckles. "Whether it's in a year or thirty, I want our children to see us openly talking. I want them to know we value what they have to say and aren't afraid to talk about hard things."

I sit up on my elbow. Amelia looks perfectly ruffled. "You've been thinking about that a lot?"

"Maybe. Ever since we changed, I've been thinking about everything. My world—our world—is moving on to a new chapter, with us as the main characters."

"What do you mean?"

"Erin. There's no denying we are special. I'd have said that before all this, but now we are special to other people besides us. The Fallen seek you out. The cured revere you. Together, we are evolving. Into what? I don't know. But it would be naive to think we can go back to our normal lives."

"But I don't want to be revered, Amelia. I'm happy to help, but I just want to get married and work at the bar. Living our lives."

"And I wish you still could, but I fear it's impossible. Mohan will have to bring the council up to speed. I would hazard a guess that new elections will be held."

"Why? What has this got to do with elections?"

I can feel my pulse steadily increasing. I don't want any of this.

"Because the people will want change. Erin, don't you see? For the first time in our history, we can save vampires from a fate worse than death. The community will want the old system updated."

"What old system?"

"Mohan and the other Grand Masters' system of keeping everyone safe. That's been their winning formula because that's all vampires needed. Keeping the Fallen at bay and protecting regular vampire citizens is the reason Mohan and the other Grand Masters win elections."

"That hasn't changed at all, Amelia. Humans still don't know we exist. There is still a need for safety. Their winning formula is still firmly in place."

"Yes, but now we don't need protecting from our own kind. The more outspoken vampires will want to see change. Growth. This movement to have vampires come out will only pick up more steam now the Fallen vampires are no longer a threat."

"Mohan can lead the way."

"Yes, but, and I'm only guessing, you and I will be seen as figureheads. The Salvator Regina and her protector."

"That's absurd."

"But likely. Just like humans, vampires love a symbol or a person to levy upon a stool to idolize. And the fact they will have a queen once more will only add to the calls for reform. Remember, vampires are different from humans. They value women in power. Which I know seems hypercritical considering the majority of our Grand Masters are men, but even those in power will happily step aside for you to be their queen. "

"We're not gods, Amelia. Just variants of our kind. That's it."

"It doesn't matter. Erin, you saw how the cured vampires reacted to you. In their eyes, you *are* a queen."

I sit up, slumping against the headboard. Is Amelia right?

"Why did we have to talk about all this? I was in a blissfully sated sex bubble."

"I'm sorry, my love. I certainly do *not* want to take you from our sex bubble. But I want us to talk and think about our future. I want to marry you, Erin, and have children. But I want us to do all that with a clear idea of what our future may entail."

I'm being stubborn, I know that. Funny really considering how adaptable I usually am. It's not like finding out the woman you're seeing is a vampire—wasn't life-altering. So why could I deal with that, but not this?

"I'm sorry." I sigh. "I'm just finding all of this very hard to digest."

"I know, and we'll get through it. Sometimes things are out of our control. Just like us falling in love. Things can be inevitable."

"And you believe our thrust into the vampire community spotlight is inevitable?"

Amelia kneels in front of me and takes my face in her palms. "I think it is. But whatever happens, we have each other. I'll be right by your side."

Our conversation continues to slip in and out of focus as

the day progresses. We finally make it out of bed around lunchtime, after more sex and some much-needed sleep.

Mohan's urgent request that we meet him and the council at the Loch residence isn't sitting well. I feel Amelia's predictions are about to come true.

"Want to take the Ducati?"

I smile excitedly at Amelia. That's exactly what I want.

"Yes, let's take the coastal road."

Suiting up in all our leathers, I take a second to appreciate Amelia in all-black leather. Mmm, she's delicious.

Hammering the throttle, I let out a squeak of elation, gripping Amelia's waist tighter. We weave through LA traffic with ease. The rush is exhilarating. Amelia is throwing caution to the wind as we tear through the city.

The ever-beautiful sight of the ocean brings me a sense of calm, even at our alarming speed. Unfortunately, we have to turn off far too soon.

The Loch mansion looms over us as we drive up. The front of the property is, as usual, packed with cars. This means we are the last to arrive.

Amelia swings the bike into a space close to the main door. Victoria is there to greet us.

"Hello, my loves." She kisses us both, wrapping an arm around each of our shoulders, escorting us to the kitchen. I should have put money on all the Lochs being seated at their Mafia-style table. The sight never fails to make me smile.

However, today there are several additions. Mohan being one, the council members being the other, sans Noah, obviously.

"Wonderful," Mohan exclaims. "We can call this meeting to order."

"May I ask what we're meeting about?" Laurence asks.

"The future," Mira, a beautiful Indian vampire, states clearly. "Mohan has brought us all up to speed on recent developments. It's good to see you and Amelia are well, Erin."

I nod and smile. I knew Victoria planned to inform Mohan of my miraculous escape from death and her daughter's stupidity. Her words.

"We're here to discuss how we move forward," Mohan adds.

"In what way?" I ask.

I already know what's coming. Amelia will earn the right to say, "I told you so!"

"As we are all aware, there has been increased chatter from the community, expressing their desire to reveal our species to humans." Mohan pauses to look each of us in the eye. "Until now, I have vocally disagreed."

"You wish for us to come out?" Harlan asks.

I sit quietly, taking a drink from the glass of Red sitting in front of me.

"I want a discussion. If we are to consider it, we need a plan. It's not as simple as announcing our existence. I think we all know that."

Yeah, we do. It would be utterly stupid. Humans don't have a reputation for welcoming *each other's* differences, let alone a new species they already fear. I'm with Amelia on that. Amazing how we seem to have reversed our original opinions. Amelia is all for springing out of the closet, and now I'm the one who is far more wary.

Louis, another member of the council, sits forward. "I believe it prudent to inform the community of Erin and Amelia's unique abilities. Let them decide if it has a bearing on who leads them."

"I concur," Mohan adds.

"Hold on. You're getting ahead of yourselves. Amelia and I are only just figuring out these new abilities. We're not politicians. Neither of us has a desire to lead anyone. Surely that's our decision, not the council's or the community's?"

Several of the Lochs nod their heads in agreement. Victoria places her glass down and wipes her mouth before speaking in that matronly voice I admire.

"Things may change, Mohan, but we still need a political leader. We still need the council. Surely, Erin and Amelia could be mere figureheads. I understand the community will warm to them. After all, they're able to do something no one else, that we can verify, has ever done. But thrusting them into leading is unfair and could cause more harm."

"I agree," Amelia emphasizes. "At the heart of all this, Erin and I were given these abilities to help our fellow vampires. A task, I may add, that is taxing on us both. I won't speak for my mate, but I will say this. I'm happy to help humans find their immortality. And I will do so proudly. That is what I want to focus on. That and finally marrying Erin."

Taking her hand, I kiss her on the cheek. "I'm with Amelia. I want to help the Fallen. Mohan, you and the council are the best vampires for this job."

"Would you consider liaising with us then?" Mira asks. "If we can show the community you are involved in decisions relating to our future, I think we would stand a better chance of pleasing everyone."

Amelia and I look at each other. "Yes," we chorus.

"We can do that," I add.

Mohan smiles and nods. "That's a start. Now to the more pressing matter."

"Noah." All eyes turn to me as I say his name.

"Noah," Mohan echoes. "The doctor is no longer a threat. Many of the vampires involved have been taken into custody. Only Noah and a handful of his men are still at large."

It's thanks to Jordan and Chris that Dr. Mendhi is no longer a player in the game. I felt the burning desire for revenge coursing through their very cells as they surrounded his home. They found him desperately trying to burn evidence of his wicked ways before subduing him. It took Chris an enormous amount of self-control not to rip his throat out. Of course, because of our connection, I felt every second of his internal struggle.

Truth be told, I wouldn't have blamed him if he'd allowed his vengeance to seek justice. However, he chose a different path. Chris handed Dr. Mendhi over to Mohan's security team. I'm assured the Doctor will be treated humanely, but will never again see the light of day. I wonder if he knows the damage he caused. The pain and fear Chris and Jordan still relive daily through their memories.

"And how do you plan to capture him, Mohan?" Aliah asks.

"With us," I announce, to my own surprise.

Twenty-Eight

Mom always said I have an internal bullshit switch. A fail-safe to stop myself from getting hurt. I laughed it off, but in the end I think she's right. Of course I worry and get anxious like everyone. I get upset and things hurt me, but then I get to a point where I simply can't stand feeling that way anymore and my switch flips.

Instead of being on the defensive, I pivot and fight back. It's like my mind can only take so much suffering and then it shifts into pro-active mode. I work out what is causing me anxiety and pain and then I deal with it. I throw everything I have into making the situation better.

Noah is causing me anxiety, and I'm over it. That asshat already shot me once and I'm done. Right now he's running around thinking he's the biggest, baddest vampire out there. He's wrong. There are two vampires that are about to lay his ass out.

I think my fighting talk could do with some work.

Anyway, now my switch has flicked, I'm able to see past my fears. My rational mind is back in the driver's seat and I can see things clearly. My abilities alone aren't enough to stop Noah. He has the power to stop me from manipulating his mind. But he hasn't accounted for Amelia.

I understand now what she meant by declaring that her purpose is to protect me. But she's wrong about one thing. Her ability is there to protect us both, I'm sure of it. From the moment we bonded, something spectacular occurred. We operate better as one, so it stands to reason that together, Amelia and I can beat Noah. We are an unstoppable force.

"Care to explain?" Mohan asks after my declaration.

I look at Amelia and see the recognition in her eyes. She knows I'm finally seeing things clearly.

"Amelia and I have extraordinary abilities. Together, I believe we can end this. I want to summon him. The fact I'm not dead will put him on the back foot."

Mohan sits forward. "You want to draw him out, and what?"

Amelia stands, her palms resting on the tabletop. "Arrest him."

"Surely you can provide security to help with his followers. Amelia and I will do the rest."

"How?" Mira asks.

Standing, I circle Amelia's waist. "By trusting in our bond."

The group spends several minutes talking amongst themselves. Amelia and I converse silently. We are finally on the same page. There's no need to plan. We will know what to do when the time comes.

"The council agrees. Erin and Amelia will tackle Noah. We will move the cured vampires to a secure location until the threat is neutralized.

"I'll start making the arrangements," Mira states, already excusing herself, phone in hand.

"Unless you are essential or a part of the security force, I must ask you to leave."

Mohan's demand is met with uproar from the Loch siblings.

"Silence," Harlan bellows. "The Grand Master has spoken."

This is the first time I've seen Harlan put his foot down. The family falls silent. Some of them even drop their eyes to the table.

"We all have a role to play. Even if that means staying out of the way," he states.

"The cured vampires will need all the help they can get," Amelia adds. "While we deal with Noah, could you all step up? Help them?"

Her gaze scans her siblings.

"We'll do our part. Just be careful." Lucille stands. "Come on, let's get to it. I want to get back to my husband and son at some point this century."

Following Lucille's lead, the rest of the clan make their way out, stopping to wish us well and give hugs. It's quite the emotional display, and one I could do without. I need my head in fight mode.

Understanding my need to stay in the right frame of mind, Amelia is all business. "Where do you want to do this?"

"I'll reach out and invite him here. I doubt he'll try the sneaky way this time."

"You think he's going to come in guns blazing?"

"Probably. That way, he could get more than just me. He'll be hoping to take down as many as possible."

Amelia nods. "Well, no time like the present."

I love Amelia's unshakable resolve and calm. We're about to do something extremely dangerous, on a hunch that we can actually protect ourselves from vampires with guns. And here she is, my beautiful mate, talking as if we're about to go grocery shopping.

"Okay. Here goes nothing."

Reaching into my mind, I search for Noah's tainted light. A smile forms when I link to him. His shock is so strong, it's like he's here in the room with me.

Not wanting to stay in his head any longer than necessary, I send my simple message. It's something along the lines of, "Come and get me, asshole."

His rage is evident. I doubt we'll have to wait long.

"Get everyone into place. Tell your parents to stay inside."

"They're not going to like that, my love."

"We need to concentrate. They'll understand."

Amelia nods and sets off to find Victoria and Harlan. I take advantage of being alone for a few seconds. This could go wrong. Amelia and I haven't tested our abilities together yet. My mind wanders to my parents. I make the snap decision to reach out to them. I doubt they'll understand

I'm in their heads. But it doesn't matter. I want them to know I'm thinking of them.

"I'm sure they heard you, honey." Amelia's voice makes me jump. "We'll see them soon."

Shaking off any last anxiety, I stand tall. Well, as tall as possible. "Are you ready?"

"I'm ready. Shall we greet our guests outside?"

The security team is dotted around the entrance and outside the main doors. We descend the stone steps, walking a little further away from the house. The day is slipping by in a haze of summer light. Closing my eyes, I listen to the birds. The rustle of the leaves as a slight breeze passes through.

"Do you hear that?" Amelia asks. Cocking my head, I zero in on engines.

"Yes, I hear them."

All of Noah's previous calm and confidence is missing when he steps out of the Range Rover. His eyes scour over me. I bet he's trying to decide if this is some sort of trick. I doubt he can fathom the idea that there is someone more powerful than him. That's the type of arrogance he embodies.

A dozen vampires exit the other cars, which have pulled up beside Noah's. They all look like they spend their lives lifting weights. Strength is more than muscle, as Noah and his friends are about to find out.

"Well," he drawls, "this is a surprise."

"Isn't it just! Seems I have a few tricks up my sleeve neither of us were aware of last night."

I feel pure hatred rolling off Amelia. Her body is rigid, and I know she's struggling to keep her more vengeful side under control.

"Well, I'll make sure I do a better job this time." Noah is practically spitting venom as he replies.

I sense his presence, trying to penetrate my mind. Amelia takes my hand, entwining our fingers. All her anger is suddenly gone. Looking at her, I see a grin playing on her face. Noah looks from me to Amelia, his brow furrowing.

And then I understand. His attempts to connect with me are failing. I feel Amelia's influence. This is the protection she was talking about. Somehow, she's thrown a shield around both our minds. Noah has no influence.

He's realizing what I already know. Without his ability to lock us in our own minds, he is vulnerable. That's the only weapon in his arsenal. With a flick of his wrist, his buddies draw out their weapons, causing the security team behind us to mirror them.

So he plans to mow us down in a shower of bullets.

"Not if I can help it," Amelia whispers. The surrounding air shimmers. Her hand clenches mine as a current runs through our bodies. I see Noah and his men watching in disbelief. Gold and blue strings of light wind their way from our joined hands.

Buzzing shrouds my hearing. Amelia's body is almost vibrating as she emits blue light. My body is warming. Looking down, my breath falters—I'm glowing gold. Snapping my head to my mate, I gasp. Our lights are radiating, swirling, joining. They dance around, forming a protective layer.

Noah screams directions to his men. I hear guns fire, but I feel no pain. The raw power flowing through us is almost overwhelming. No shots are getting through. It's time to end this. My mind snatches control of Noah's with such ease I want to laugh. There is nothing for him to do. I have him trapped.

I continue my assault by snaring the minds of his men. *Put the weapons down.* My voice rings clear and strong. Without hesitation, they relinquish their guns. The clatter of metal hitting the ground signals the security team to rush forward. In the distance, I hear someone shout, "Clear!"

Letting go of their minds is easy. It's Noah's I'm having trouble releasing. Something deep inside me wants to make him suffer, like he did to all those vampires over the decades. Why shouldn't he feel their pain? It would be so easy to do.

Come back, my love. Amelia's voice coats my anger, smothering it until the flames have died out. I won't hurt him, but I will render him incapable of using his abilities again.

Speaking to Amelia through the ether, I ask for her help. Together, we bind Noah's ability. I couldn't tell you how we are able to do it. Just that I knew we could. As soon as I am sure we've succeeded, I let go.

The world comes into view. There are no more lights, just Amelia and I holding hands, breathing hard. In front of us, Noah and his team are face down on the ground, their hands tied behind their backs.

"Amelia, Erin!" Victoria races toward us, tugging us into a behemoth hug. My feet lift slightly as the much taller woman heaves me into her. "My god," she gasps. "I couldn't believe what I was seeing." Her voice breaks slightly with emotion.

I can't quite believe what we did, to be honest. I knew we would be powerful together, but that was something else.

No sooner am I let go from Victoria's arms, than I'm scooped up into Harlan's.

"You did it," he bellows, momentarily deafening me.

"Harlan," I mutter into his chest. My face is completely buried in him as he squeezes me.

"Oh, sorry, my dear." He chuckles, finally letting me breathe. Amelia smiles as she is given the same treatment. Although at least her head reaches her father's shoulder.

There is a flurry of activity as more cars arrive. Mohan and the council, plus the rest of the Loch Clan, pour out of their respective vehicles. Were they on speed dial?

"I called them as soon as Noah showed up," Victoria says, surrounding me with her long arms again.

Mohan touches my arm whilst looking up at Amelia. "Is everyone okay?"

Amelia nods. "We're fine."

"They're more than fine," Harlan proclaims. "They're Salvator Regina."

To my utter embarrassment, Harlan drops to his knee, bowing his head. My head whips to Amelia. I'm begging her to do something, but she just stands there, head held high. Victoria is the next to drop. One by one, every vampire except the ones handcuffed are on their knees, heads bowed.

Twenty-Nine

M y palms are sweating outrageously. It makes me sad that I'm this nervous before a visit to my parents. We were always a close-knit family, able to talk about anything. I just hope we can get past this.

Amelia wanted to come with me. In fact, the discussion almost turned into a fight when I told her I wanted to do this alone. Since our awakening—that's what we're referring to the event that happened last week—our bond has intensified, something neither of us thought possible. Something ancient runs through our veins. Both of us have heightened senses. My strength and speed almost match Amelia's, although her reflexes and awareness are unparalleled.

Even though we are navigating this new reality together, I need to figure things out with Mom and Dad alone. I'll let her pout for a few hours before I unashamedly use my womanly charms to entice her out of her sulking.

But now I have to focus. Standing outside my parents' front door isn't getting me anywhere. I just need to bite the bullet and knock. My hand freezes midway to the door. What if they turn me away? I don't know what I will do.

"Erin?" My mother's voice ricochets through me. Turning, we stare, unable to speak. Only then do I see how many bags of groceries she's trying to juggle. Rushing forward—far too fast for any human—I take two bags.

"Here, let me help."

I daren't look in her eyes. I know she sees the difference in me. There are a few awkward moments of silence before Mom pulls herself together and lets us into the house.

The fresh smell of coffee and cinnamon hits me in the heart. I've missed their smell. I've missed the comfort of coming home. Mom sets her bags down and starts putting the food away.

"Where's Dad?"

"Golf."

"When will he be home?"

"Oh, any second I would imagine."

Wow, this is painful. Mom won't even look at me.

"Mom, please stop." Reaching for her shoulder, I feel her trembling. Is she scared of me? But then, in an instant, she turns and hauls me into her body. I thought I had strength. It's nothing compared to a mother's strength when she needs her kid close, apparently.

"Mom," I gasp, "I can't breathe."

"Oh, Erin, I'm so sorry." Tears are pouring down her face. There is nothing worse than seeing your mom cry. Well, maybe your Dad. Which is about to happen as I look over Mom's shoulder, seeing my dad standing in all his golf gear with tears brimming in his eyes.

"Dad," I croak, because goddammit I'm choking up.

"Sweetie." He sniffs, walking over with purpose. He slips his arms around us both, hugging us tightly. I inhale both of them and let my heart heal for a second. We still need to talk, and they might not be so happy I'm back once they know what's been going on lately.

"Coffee, we need coffee," Mom chatters, pulling herself away.

We all take a few beats to get ourselves into a reasonable state. Dad sits at the table pulling over a steaming cup—of way too thick—coffee. I'm finally going to buy Mom that coffee pod machine after this conversation. Depending on how it goes.

"We're sorry, Erin," Dad begins. "We reacted badly and said some things neither of us are proud of, sweetie. You're our little girl, and we got scared, but instead of supporting you, we lashed out."

Putting my hand over his, I take a seat next to him. "That day was terrifying for everyone. I understand why you were upset."

"What...what's happened to you since?" Mom sits now, too. Her hands shake as she caresses my face. "You look different."

"Because I am. Will you let me show you?"

Sitting forward, Dad searches my face. Almost like he's mapping every discrepancy. "How?"

"Trust me, and close your eyes."

They share a quick look but do as I ask. Hopefully, they won't completely lose it once they see the truth. If they thought learning vampires exist was far-fetched, wait until they get a load of the past few weeks.

I ease into their minds, not wanting to frighten them. I feel Mom jump slightly when she feels my presence. Starting from the day they left the Loch mansion, I play back everything I've been through until last week.

A whoosh of air leaves their lungs as I retreat from their consciousness. Dad stares at me with wide eyes, while Mom remains frozen, her eyes still shut tight.

"Erin...you're...this—"

"It's a lot. But I need you to know the truth. I'm still your daughter, just a little...different."

Dad gasps. "You're a vampire queen?"

I wince visually.

"You're not a queen? Did I get that wrong?" His apologetic tone makes me smile through the awkwardness.

"That's what people are calling me, us. I'm still getting used to it."

"It does sound rather fantastical," he comments.

"It sounds nuts." I laugh. He chuckles along with me. Turning my attention to my mom, I place my hand on her forearm. "Mom?"

Opening her eyes, she looks at my dad and then at me. "It's...well. Wow!"

"The transformation took us all by surprise. Hell, the entire situation threw us."

"Amelia, she's changed too?"

"Well, she's a vampire like before, just a little more—"

"Juiced," Dad replies.

"Yeah."

Silence rains down and I let it happen. They've just received a hell of a shock and I can't let history repeat itself. I can't let them walk away from me.

Running a hand through her hair, Mom nods to herself. "We need to apologize to Amelia and the rest of the family."

"Yes, you're right," Dad agrees.

My heart stutters. "So...does this mean we're okay?"

My voice sounds a lot smaller than usual.

Taking my head in her hands, Mom smiles and cries again. Dad puts his hand on my shoulder and squeezes.

"Yes, honey. There's no need to worry. We're alright. It will take some time to fully adapt, but you are our child and our world. We promise not to leave you like that again."

My floodgates well and truly open. A week's worth of fear and anxiety cascades down my face. Mom holds me tight, whispering loving words of support in my ear.

With a hiccup and a small cough, I sit up, look both my parents in the face and smile.

"Good, because I'm getting married in three days."

∞

"Are you sure this is what you want?" Amelia asks me for the tenth time today. Looking at the small archway erected near the rose garden, I sigh happily.

"It's perfect."

"It's tiny."

Exactly how I want it. Now Amelia and I are on every vampire's radar from LA to Tokyo. I want us to be married immediately. No more waiting. As soon as Mohan uttered the words "public wedding" I shot into action. It's one thing adapting to a new way of life, constantly being surrounded by people. It's another sharing intimate moments. Our wedding is for us, and us alone. Which is why the only people invited are the Lochs, my parents, Jordan, Mack, and Chris. I politely asked the council not to attend.

Anya and Barty agreed to stand as witnesses for us. Neither of us could think of any two people more suited. Barty and Anya have been invaluable these past few weeks. Barty scoured every library, every private collection, and spoke to every vampire who may give us answers. In the end, we had to conclude that the ancient queen was real, her partner also. There are too many eyewitness accounts and testimony for her to be a myth. However, together we weeded out the fantasy, stripped the tales down to the bare bones.

None of us are sure how Amelia and I inherited our abilities. But what does it matter? We have them and are both ready to serve the Fallen and their mates. But before we give our lives to service, I want us to have one day, our wedding day, completely to ourselves.

"I want to be your wife, Amelia. I couldn't care less about flower arrangements or seating plans. We've already waited too long."

"We were waiting for your thirtieth."

"And now we don't have to. God knows what other shit life will throw at us."

Slipping her hand around my neck, Amelia ducks her head to look me in the eye. "Whatever comes our way, we're in it together, my queen."

I can't stop the blush from overtaking my face. When Amelia calls me her queen in her low, sexy voice, I melt from the feet up.

"Yes, together," I utter stupidly because my focus is less on word formation than it is on getting her lips on mine.

"All right, knock it off," Anya calls. "Time to take your places."

"I'll see you soon," Amelia whispers in my ear, brushing her lips just below. A shiver runs through me.

I'm jerked from her proximity before I have a chance to respond. Anya laughs when I scowl at her playfully.

"If I didn't take action, you'd be there all day saying goodbye even though you're about to marry the woman in five minutes."

We pass our families heading to the arch. Anya drags me to the closest powder room and begins fluffing. "You look gorgeous!"

"Thank you. Amelia looks delicious."

Anya laughs again. "She is very striking."

"Can we go now?"

Shaking her head, Anya beams at me. "Yes, dear Erin, we can go now. Amelia should be in place."

Walking down the aisle is the only part of the wedding Amelia insisted on. Taking a deep breath, I do my level best not to sprint back to the garden. A solo violinist begins to play, and everyone turns to me. My eyes are only on Amelia. It's finally happening.

We definitely walk quicker than the tempo of the "Wedding March," which causes a few titters amongst the Loch clan. I barely notice when Anya squeezes my hand and kisses me on the cheek, followed by Barty. Claire steps forward, ready to commence the ceremony. She was delighted when Amelia asked her to officiate. It took her a matter of minutes to grab her laptop and get ordained online.

Clearing her throat, Claire looks between us. "Shall we get you two hitched?"

"Yes, please," I reply. Amelia tugs me forward and plants a deep kiss on my lips.

I hear a distant, "Oh, for fuck's sakes," from Lucille.

Claire flicks Amelia on the ear, causing her to retreat with a small, "Ow."

"Right. Stop skipping bits and I won't have to hurt you."

Rolling my lips in to hide my snigger, I take Amelia's hands. "Can I say my vows now?"

Claire rolls her eyes. "Why the hell not?"

The small crowd chuckles.

Taking one of my hands, I lay it on Amelia's chest, above her heart. The other hand, I place over my own.

"Amelia, you are mine, and I yours. We are bonded for eternity. Our vows made and consummated. There are no words that can relay my true feelings. But I know you feel them, every day. I love you, Amelia Loch, with all that I am and all that I will be. You are my strength, my grace, and my soul. I will treasure you forever."

"I have no vows," Amelia begins, her stature strong and proud. "Words are not enough. I will show you in every action I take what you mean to me, my love. Forever."

Again she pulls me in and kisses me.

"Jesus, okay, I guess we're at the kissing part. Do you both take each other to be lawfully wedded wives?"

We both mutter, "Yes" through the kiss.

"I'll take that as a yes, then," Claire continues. "In the power vested in me by the internet, I now pronounce you wife and wife. Can someone please pass me a drink?"

Howls and hollers pierce the air. Amelia picks me up off my feet, diving into my mouth with her tongue. Wrapping my legs around her waist, I feel us moving. Wolf whistles and catcalls follow us into the house. I guess Amelia's ready to start the honeymoon.

Epilogue

I roll over for what must be the tenth time in as many minutes. The air is thick with wet heat, and the fan is doing little to aid in our comfort. A frustrated sigh escapes my lips. Wincing, I turn slowly to peer at Amelia. The moonlight reflects in her eyes as she stares at me.

"We'll know soon enough," she whispers.

I wish her words would soothe me. God knows I could do with the rest. This is our first night in Hawaii. We're finally taking our honeymoon, six months after the wedding. The day after we said yes to becoming wives, our lives have been a nonstop whirlwind of activity.

The world's vampire governments began sending their Fallen over to us in LA. Can you imagine the chaos it caused? Eventually, Mohan set up a shelter to house them all, and to give Amelia and me a place to work. For weeks, Riley milked me. Taking as much serum from my fangs as possible.

Amelia fared better, as there were only a handful of human mates that required her skills. Yet, she is just as exhausted as me. We've been navigating politics and true believers. Vampires who wish to worship us as queens. Something I've tried my hardest to avoid, but am yet to succeed.

Our ascension has been rapid and overwhelming, which is why Amelia flew us to paradise for a few weeks. Especially considering Mohan is in the middle of telling the president of the United States that vampires are real. Neither of us wanted to stick around for that.

And yet, here I am, unable to sleep because my thoughts are with him. I try my damnedest to stay out of people's minds, but tonight I'm struggling. Mohan's apprehension and anxiety are palpable to me. I have no idea where he'll begin explaining all of this.

"I wish I could just shut it off," I grumble.

"Maybe I can help with that?" Amelia rolls on top of me, and I'd be lying if I said her methods were ineffective.

"Yes, this could work."

Since marrying, we have certainly lived up to the "honeymoon phase." We stayed in the penthouse for a solid forty-eight hours after the wedding. Of course, we shared a drink and some cake with the family straight after the ceremony. Okay, not *straight* after. Amelia had other ideas, and we were late for the toasts. But once our obligations were done, Amelia took us home on her Ducati, and that's where we stayed for two days.

Lucille eventually shattered our bubble, in the rudest way possible. She burst into our bedroom mid-orgasm with a foghorn. Amelia nearly hit the roof when the wretched thing blasted through the room. I've never seen her so close to killing her sister.

Then, it was down to business. The council consulted with other vampire leaders around the world and came to a consensus: it was time to reveal our identity.

Victoria and Harlan sat through many of their meetings on our behalf. We made our feelings clear about not revealing Amelia and me as some sort of deities. We already felt revealing our species was going to be tricky enough. Add in vampire queens, and we're just asking for trouble. Let's not kid ourselves, men in power tend to feel threatened easily.

"Erin, my love, come back. You're wandering from me."

"I'm sorry, honey."

"It's okay. Look, whatever happens, we're prepared."

"Are we? We have no idea what the hell is going to happen. We're banking on the president being a forward-thinking kind of woman. But this... Amelia, finding out vampires exist is—"

"Is nuts, as you so eloquently like to phrase it. But the councils have agreed. It's happening."

"Oh, I know it is. I can sense Mohan's heart rate from here." I laugh.

"Then will you let me love you? Mother will call as soon as Mohan is back from DC. Let's just have these peaceful, precious few hours to indulge in us."

"You're right." Grabbing her ass, I pull her closer to me. "Touch me, and make everything good again, even if it's just for a little while."

Brushing her nose gently against mine, Amelia teases me with her mouth. Her tongue flicks out, swiping across my bottom lip. My breath is already coming faster as her hips settle between my legs.

"You're wet already."

"Of course I am. Look at my wife."

That earns a smirk. Massaging her backside, I moan when she grinds harder. Sleeping naked has many benefits, one being less time to get down and dirty when the feeling strikes. Her soft curls brush against mine, the coarse hair creating friction.

"Oh baby, that's damn good," I breathe into the night. Amelia's head is snug against my neck as she picks up the pace.

"Do you want to come like this?"

"Yes, and then with your mouth."

My clit pulses as the orgasm builds. Climaxing like this is one of my favorite ways to come. Amelia's powerful body on mine, her skin gliding over me. Her breath close to my ear, and her heart pounding next to mine. I also love her ass and I know it drives her wild when I grab it as she fucks me.

"Erin," she gasps.

I can't answer because my mind is consumed by radiating pleasure. The usual gold and blue lights shimmer around us as we tumble helplessly off the edge. Our combined shouts of joy echo around the silent room.

"God, I love it when we do that."

"Then let's do it some more." Amelia lifts herself slightly and moves down my body. Maybe I don't need as much sleep as I thought.

∞

Something isn't right. I'm asleep, but my visions are real. I know it. There's so much blood. My head is turned, and Amelia is lying beside me, her lifeless eyes staring at nothing. All the air in my lungs vanishes in a second. I hear myself screaming her name, but she doesn't move. Then, a voice that isn't my own snakes through my subconscious... It's Amelia.

"Erin, Erin!"

My body convulses.

"Erin, wake up!"

The vision is suddenly gone, replaced by Amelia's concerned and very alive eyes. I need air, but I can't seem to get my body to respond.

"Baby, breathe, just breathe."

I listen to the calming tone of her voice and command myself to take in air.

Gasping and gulping, I fill my lungs. "Amelia," I choke. "Something isn't right."

And then I hear it. A creak from the door to our suite opening. Amelia's keen senses pick up on it too. Her head cocks slightly to listen.

Silently she beckons me to move to the wall shared with the bedroom door. We are both naked but on high alert. Someone is in the living room. Actually, there are several someones trying to creep through the suite. Obviously, they aren't aware of how hard it is to sneak up on two highly evolved vampires.

We bide our time. My body tenses, readying for a fight as the bedroom door slowly opens. The tip of a gun pokes through. Amelia is watching like a hawk ready to strike her prey. The door opens fully and four armed men in tactical gear stalk in. Their weapons aimed at the bed.

The lead man raises his fist, halting the others. He scans the room but doesn't look our way. We are shrouded in darkness, watching and waiting. I'll have to thank Chris and Jordan for the hiding-on-a-ceiling idea.

"They're not here," the leader announces, his voice full of hate.

"Well, where the fuck are they?" another asshole asks.

"We're here, motherfuckers," Amelia growls, and then she's gone from my side, dropping to the floor. I wait patiently as Amelia takes care of our guests. They never saw her coming.

Tiptoeing my way through incapacitated bodies, I slip on my robe, handing Amelia's to her. "Cover up, honey."

"Thanks," she mumbles, tying the robe quickly. She searches each man, taking their weapons.

Bending down, I look into the leader's fearful eyes. Each of them is bound and gagged but conscious.

"And who might you be?"

"Fuck you, bitch."

His garbled words earn him a swift kick to the nuts courtesy of my wife.

"They're U.S. military," Amelia says through gritted teeth. I look at the clock on the wall. It's been six and a half hours since Mohan spoke to the president.

"We need to call home," I state. Tossing Amelia her phone, I close my eyes and reach out to Mohan. We need answers.

I connect almost immediately, like he was waiting for me.

We've been attacked.

The only message I receive sends shivers down my spine.

We were wrong to tell them.

And then silence.

Amelia and Erin's journey continues in *Fighting for Infinity*.

Afterword

Thank you for reading Waiting for Eternity.
Please spare a few more minutes of your time by heading
over to Amazon and Goodreads to leave a review.

Other Titles By Alyson Root

A Dance Towards Forever

Diving Into Her

Always Emilie

The Misadventures of Callie Compton

Broken Parts Included

Love & Other Wild Things

Finding Molly Parsons

Keeping Carmen Ruiz

The Wisdom of Bug

Sleigh Bells Ring

Risking Immortality

Waiting for Eternity
Fighting for Infinity

About the author

Alyson was born and raised in the heart of England. She moved to Paris in 2015 when she met her wife. Together they moved to the west of France, where they now live with their two dogs. Alyson spends her time reading sapphic fiction books, writing and Scuba Diving.

Alyson discovered her love of writing in her mid-thirties. Her debut book, *A Dance Towards Forever,* was inspired by her wife and their very own love story. Alyson wrote *Diving Into Her* and award-winning *Always Emilie,* which added with her first book, created The French Connection series.

www.alysonroot.com

a.rootauthor@alysonroot.com

www.ingramcontent.com/pod-product-compliance
Lightning Source LLC
Chambersburg PA
CBHW030552170726
48283CB00002B/288